Joy Outweighs the Sorrow

A Novel

by

Bonnie Holt

This book is not an official publication of The Church of Jesus Christ of Latter-day Saints. All opinions expressed herein are those of the author's and are not necessarily those of the publisher's or of The Church of Jesus Christ of Latter-day Saints.

Published and distributed by:

GRANITE PUBLISHING & DISTRIBUTION

270 S. Mountainlands Dr.
Orem, UT 84058
(801) 229-9023

ISBN: 0-9644552-8-5
Library of Congress Catalog Card Number: 95-71683

Cover Design by:
Jerilynn Carter

Page layout and design by:
SUNRISE PUBLISHING
(801) 224-7270

Author's Note

Although the characters in this book are fiction—they live. Perhaps you will recognize the kindness of Mr. Hansen, the despair of Emma, or the fear and prejudice of Sharon's mother. I know you all know Jack Carlson—everyone knew a *Jack* in sixth grade! And the character of Marie was based on my own experiences growing up as an inactive member of the Church of Jesus Christ of Latter-day Saints.

I was baptized at the usual age of eight, but had never attended church nor understood anything of my religion until, as a shy, frightened little girl, I crouched in a corner behind the old wood stove and listened as the missionaries taught my nonmember stepfather the gospel. He was never interested, but I knew they spoke the truth!

The testimony I gained then of my Savior Jesus Christ has been the source of my Joy! Today I have been blessed with a wonderful husband and five beautiful children. We reside in Sandy, Utah, where I plan to continue writing.

Now, curl up in a comfortable chair, wrap a warm blanket around your feet, and come inside the pages. . .

Though life's sorrow's
may outnumber its joys,
the joy outweighs the sorrow!

To my daughter Rebecca
for her tender heart and enthusiasm,
who helps me remember how it feels to be almost twelve.
And to you—my friend.
Come play with me in the woods again.
We'll share secrets at recess.
We'll cry together because of the pain,
but we will also rejoice together,
because of the joy!

❦ ❦ ❦

A special thanks,
to my true blue friends:
Dianne, Kathy, Kathy, & Kathy,
Paula, Kathryn, & Kellie;
whose encouragement kept me going!
And to my husband Ron,
who in the end made this project possible!

Prologue

A full moon shone through the sheer curtains of the french door, silhouetting Marie's old ballerina doll leaning against the dining room table. A gentle breeze was moving the aspen trees outside, causing the light of the full moon to flicker. It made the doll appear to move in a slow jerking motion, seeming to dance in time to the melody of the trees, like an old silent black and white movie. But instead of piano music for accompaniment, the trees swooshed and whispered.

They whispered memories to Marie—memories of her childhood. Some of them were very painful, but they incessantly danced across her mind.

As the doll seemed to dance and the trees continued to whisper, they reminded her of how much she had loved to dance, and how much she had loved to climb trees when she was a child; especially with her best friend. Marie could almost smell the musty earth from their buried treasure and feel the breeze in the trees they'd climbed together . . .

"You have a funny china closet, grandma."

Five-year-old Jenni startled Marie. "What are you doing up, honey?"

"I couldn't sleep," and before Marie could reply Jenni

continued, "our china closet has dishes. Why does yours have dolls in it?"

Without letting her grandma get a word in edgewise Jenni kept asking questions, "Grandma, why is the light off?"

Marie knew she was sitting in the dark because she couldn't sleep. She had intended to have a snack and then go back to bed, but her ballerina doll standing by the door had caught her eye, so she sat down to watch her dance in the moonlight. The unexpected return of her old ballerina doll that afternoon had brought back so many memories.

But to Jenni she merely said, "I don't know—I think the moonlight is pretty coming through the window."

"It scares me."

Just then Jenni's mother walked into the room and flipped on the light saying, "Then, we'll get you a drink and off to bed you go."

"But—I wanna' see grandma's dolls."

"Not now Jenni. It's time for bed!"

To Marie's surprise, Jenni gave *her* a kiss and her mother a mean look, but obediently ran off to bed.

"I certainly couldn't get my children to mind that well."

Dianne just smiled and Marie said, "Couldn't you sleep either?"

"No, and I'm so tired. But you know how a strange bed and house are."

"Yes, I remember when I used to stay with my in-laws when we'd come in from California. How fun it was traveling with babies. We didn't even have paper diapers! Would you like a snack?"

Without waiting for a reply, Marie poured her

daughter-in-law a glass of juice and buttered some bagels.

As she began to eat, Dianne said, "It's so odd, isn't it, that your cousin sent your ballerina doll back after all these years."

Marie picked up her old doll and touched her matted blonde hair reverently, then examined the doll's right hand as she explained to Dianne, "My Uncle Jack's dog, Popcorn, chewed her fingers off when I was six years old."

She walked over to her china closet and stood the doll on the ledge, leaning her against the glass. "I guess it's time to look for a better display case for my dolls. My old ballerina is too large to fit inside."

"Your dolls are so unique and beautiful. Whenever I see your Cinderella or Snow White, I remember my big sister reading those stories to me when I was a child. But the bride and groom doll are the most beautiful of all.

"I don't know too much about your fairy-tale dolls, except that they mean a great deal to you. How did you get them?"

Marie intended to give Dianne a brief accounting of the story—but the return of her ballerina doll, coupled with a willing audience, evoked too many memories. They were both oblivious to the chimes of the clock in the den, as Marie conjured up the image of an unhappy little girl perched in a wide crook of an old apple tree . . .

Chapter One

At first glance the young girl, sitting in the grand old apple tree, was as silent and still as the rest of nature on that hot afternoon. Even her hair, which hadn't seen a brush in a week and looked quite ready to yield to the slightest breeze, seemed perfectly frozen in its disarray. It was an unusual color, hard for most people to describe. Like a chameleon, it was moody—under artificial lights it was lemon colored, at twilight she was a towhead and now, in the bright sun, her short hair flashed with hints of strawberry red.

She was leaning back against the tree's main trunk dressed in cotton short-shorts and a sleeveless blouse, wrinkled, but clean in contrast to her skinny leg, which was stretched out on a branch. Her dirty bare foot hooked around the branch holding her securely in place, while her other dusty leg was propped up like an easel.

Below her scroungy patchwork cat lay drowsing in the shade of a wild rose bush—which looked as bedraggled as the cat itself. The lone bush was nestled near the porch of a small house with weathered grey clapboards, exactly matching the dominant color of the cat. In fact grey seemed to dominate the entire scene; the dirt and weeds surrounding the old house were a dry dusty grey, like the decaying sheds and corrals out back.

The only contrast was the last June rose hanging near a small patch of yellow on the sleeping cat and the green leaves of the apple tree, standing alone off to the side of the house.

The girl in the tree appeared to be as motionless as her cat sleeping in the yard below, except for her eyes. They were wide open and moving rapidly back and forth devouring a book propped on her leg. As though to defy the decree of the sun that all should be obediently still in her grey world, she earnestly escaped into a world of mystery and magic and beauty and joy.

"Ma—rie, Ma . . . rie." Like an unwelcome alarm clock interrupting a deep sleep, her mother's voice yanked the young girl so abruptly from her fantasy she nearly fell from the tree. Before she could adapt to reality, her mother's voice rent the silence again.

"Marie! Ed . . . na Ma—rie! Are you in that tree reading again when there's work to be done? I have another batch of clothes ready for you!"

After trying to climb gracefully out of the tree Marie finally jumped, picked herself up, and limp-hopped around the side of the house trying to pick stickers out of her bare feet. As she hurried, she chafed at the thought of her mother calling her *Edna.* How she hated that name. Her mother was the only one who called her Edna and she only called her Edna when she was mad or impatient or worried. These days she got called Edna a lot!

By the time she reached the back step she couldn't meet her mother's eyes, because she didn't want her to see the tears she was painfully trying to squeeze back. Marie knew her mother's impatience sprang from worry, which hurt more than the stickers in her feet.

A part of Marie wanted to shout at her mother in anger and tell her how bad it made her feel, but the tender, obedient side of her nature kept her head hung low as she walked toward the basket of clothes. As she hoisted the big basket onto her hip her eyes briefly met those of her mother.

If Marie's eyes were filled with tears, her mother's were the more to be pitied; her beautiful dark brown eyes held such a look of tired, resigned despair. They didn't speak and yet that one glance said so much.

"Marie, I'm so sorry."

"Mamma, I'm sorry! Is it my fault you are so unhappy?"

That brief moment passed as her mother silently straightened her swollen body and pressing her hand into her back, waddled back to the old farm house.

As Marie lugged the bushel basket down the dusty path toward the clothes line, she felt a noble sense of protectiveness toward her mother and was glad she hadn't added to her misery by voicing her own.

Halfway there she had to stop and pick up some of her little brother's socks that had squeezed through the hole in the side of the basket. She shook out the dust and set them off to one side. Then hung as many clothes as she could on the makeshift line she had helped her mother string between the sagging sheds behind the farmhouse. They had used old twine and even rusty bailing wire that Marie had searched out from among the rubble around the dooryard.

Soon she had to set the clean clothes aside because the lines ran out. Carefully, so she wouldn't drop them in the dust, she began to gather the dry clothes.

"Ouch, that darn line!"

Marie cried out as she snagged her thumb on a piece of rusty bailing wire where they had spliced the clothes line.

"I hate this place! I hate living in Walker and I want to move home!" Marie shouted as she stomped her foot making a little dust cloud sift into the sun.

For a second the eleven-year-old in her made her want to run to her mother for comfort, but she quickly fought down the impulse as she remembered how much her mother already had to worry about. Besides, they rarely had bandaids anyway. Instead, she rinsed her hand off in the hose and wrapped a clean sock around it, tying it with an old piece of twine lying on the ground.

She resumed her job of hanging clothes with the sun beating down on her back as she methodically hung sock after tiny sock.

Finishing the socks, she picked up her favorite school dress; it was getting much too small and she feared her mother wouldn't let her wear it again this year.

"I'll wear it anyway," she thought defiantly without too much hope of success. As Marie tenderly pinned it on the line she remembered when her mother had bought the dress.

Though her family had never had much money and never spent it on foolish things, like dancing lessons, in times past they could afford a few necessities like clothes. At least then her mother had been happy. And in those happy days, which seemed so long ago now, she had rarely called her daughter Edna! It took Marie back to the day she had learned about the significance of her first name.

"Do you know why they named you Edna?"

Marie didn't know, but she instinctively knew it was for some bad reason. She'd never liked or trusted her

Uncle Jack, who was only a few years older than Marie, and she liked him even less as she remembered how he had enjoyed telling her the secret.

"It's after yer old man." When he hadn't gotten the desired result from her blank look he continued, "You know, your dad."

When she still looked blank he had continued in disgust, "Dummy, your father. Your real father. His name was Ed and he was a real jerk. They could'a named you jerk too, but they named you Ed-na!"

In her mind Marie could still hear her uncle's laugh as he had sauntered off that day. She was only four or five years old when he'd told her that. The story had unfolded, through the years, of her horrible father who had abandoned his wife and baby. She couldn't remember him at all, but she remembered when her mother married again and they had moved into their first home.

She had been glad to move away from Uncle Jack, until she'd realized she didn't like or trust her new stepfather anymore than she had her uncle. The only man she had ever loved or trusted was her mother's father "Grandpa Daddy" and she didn't love him at all anymore, because he died and went away just like her real father had. Yes, the name Edna must mean she was not wanted, and not good enough to stay with, or pretty enough to love.

But she felt a shiver of joy as she remembered her mother's happiness and delight in her first home. She remembered how her mother had taught her to mop the floor; each crevice and corner had to be cleaned carefully. She had delighted in helping her mother make beds; not a tuck or a bump would be allowed. Her mother had painted and cleaned their little house, and acquired some modest new furniture. Marie's bedroom had been painted lemon yellow with a border of flowers all around the top.

Then her stepfather lost his job at the coal mine and her mother became worried and argued a lot with her new husband.

And then that day, just two weeks ago, she had been told they were moving because her stepfather had found a job in another town. Just remembering the abruptness of the move, and the fact that they hadn't told her in time to say goodbye to her friends, brought tears. They had sent her to spend the week with her grandma and she had arrived home to find everything packed and ready to move in the morning!

A tear spilled from her eye to think she'd never play "Kick The Can" with the Barretts across the street, or never walk to school with Debra again.

"What if I never have friends again?"

Marie shuddered even in the heat as she hung clothes and cried and remembered some more. She remembered that sad, long, last night in their pretty home. She lay in bed thinking about her mother. She would never forget the look on her face as she saw her best furniture being loaded onto a truck to be taken off and sold.

Of course none of her stepfather's stuff had been sold. He kept his statues of horses, and his horrible old deer head, which he stuck on the wall. He kept his hunting rifles and of course his television. She hated those things after that, they always reminded her of her mother's lovely lost furniture.

Her mother's furniture and *her* toys—the pain of that memory was too great, so she shut it off and wiped her damp brow with her hand. As she continued to work she tried to focus solely on hanging wet clothes, but the memories refused to be shut off so soon.

She remembered the shadows from the large old oak tree that she loved to climb, and how they had danced in the moonlight that last night. Another tear slipped away as Marie cried for that tree—sometimes she loved trees more than people. As far as Marie was concerned they all had personalities, and that old oak was grand. It had always listened to everything she had to say as she sat high and protected in its wonderful branches.

Marie swatted a fly that rebelliously dared to buzz about the hot still yard, and wiped her tears and nose on her shoulder. She knew her mother would scold her for that if she'd seen it, but just now she didn't care. Why didn't her mother tell her about the move sooner? Feelings of anger at her mother and mean stepfather for making them move to this awful place boiled inside her small breast, as she grabbed another wet shirt.

"I hate this place, I hate it!"

Marie jumped at the sound of her own voice. She looked guiltily toward the house hoping she wouldn't see her mother. As bad as she felt she'd do anything to spare her mother more pain.

Tired of the miserable direction of her thoughts, in a determined gesture Marie squared her shoulders, put her hands on her hips, and stomped her foot in the dust. She paused to watch the little dust cloud she had made sift into the sun, intrigued by the filmy patterns it made.

"Well," Marie said to no one in particular, "I can't stand being quite so sad, I'll just have to think of all the nice things about moving."

So she moved to the next clothes line and grabbed the

wet clothes with a new determination to get them hung. With a little half-smile she thought that the nicest thing would be that she wouldn't have to go to the old Grandma Giovanni's for dinner because they had moved so far away! That gave Marie true pleasure indeed.

"Now I won't have to see that fat, mean, old woman again!" She said out loud as she thought resentfully of the many times she had been made to visit her stepfather's mother. Old Grandma Giovanni, her stepfather's mother, was the fattest person Marie had ever seen in her life and she used to scare the daylights out of her.

She remembered how the old woman tried to wear her dark graying hair back in a severe bun, but wisps always managed to straggle about her plump sweaty cheeks. Marie supposed she was often sweaty from being in a hot kitchen, because she cooked the most wonderful food you could imagine.

They went to her house often for dinner and there had always been lots of aunts and uncles and cousins. For some reason she could so clearly remember the first time they had dinner there after her mother married into the family—probably because it was the first time Marie had met the old grandpa.

She was five years old and had been excited, with everyone laughing and hugging and talking. She had watched in awe behind her mother's skirts until it was time to be seated for dinner.

The big fat grandma waddled over to her mother and then looking at Marie with her small, dark eyes, spoke directly to Marie. Marie looked up at her in wonder, for she had never spoken to her before.

"Here, girl, you com'a with me." Marie still clung to

her mother and looked to her for rescue.

"It's OK, Marie, you can follow her," and with that she gave Marie a gentle push in Mrs. Giovanni's direction.

"You so slow, no need'a to be so slow." She waved her wide flabby arms toward the kitchen to hurry the child.

"Here'sa you plate, you take what you need, then you go sit on the back'a step." She handed little Marie the plate and waddled back to the dining room.

Marie wondered if the other children in the family would soon join her and so she stood for some time in the middle of the immaculate kitchen floor.

She looked up at the counter tops loaded with rolls and breadsticks, and Italian cookies dripping with honey in a myriad of interesting shapes. Her eyes moved to the stove above her and she stared for a minute at a pan. Its lid was popping gently up and down, up and down, and the thick red spaghetti sauce that stuck to it made it look like big, slobbery red lips. As the pan lid moved, it sucked on the sauce, making a smacking sound, while little rivers of red sauce trickled down the pan's chin.

The sight and smell of this wonderful food made Marie realize how very hungry she was.

Deciding not to wait for the other children, she looked up again at the counter tops and realized they were too high. Her gaze swept the room again. Looking for something to stand on, she saw a stool near the broom closet. As she began tugging at the stool it pulled loose a broom—just in time to smack a strange old man on the head, as he was entering the kitchen. He immediately began assaulting Marie with a tirade of not very pleasant sounding Italian words, while gesturing wildly in Marie's direction with the broom.

She backed off in terror! Just then in walked the fat grandma.

"What is'a going on here?" She demanded with her arms flapping.

"You—Papa, give this'a bambina her dinner!" And with that the old woman waddled back to the dining room.

Marie stared open-mouthed as the old man, muttering all the while, shuffled about the kitchen to fill her plate.

His bald old head stuck out above his stooped shoulders almost as though peeking over a wall instead of being connected. He had a bump right in the middle of his wrinkly bald forehead and his eyes were large and hung out of layers of wrinkled skin; Marie was afraid they might fall right out.

His nose was red and bulbous—it looked as though it might really honk, just like a bicycle horn, if you pinched it. He wore a black turtle neck shirt and baggy pants, which could remember better days when he had enjoyed the rich cooking of his enormous wife, but for now must be held up with bright red suspenders.

Marie watched as he generously filled her plate. As he moved from the stove to the counter, his worn, untied work boots, shuffle-clunked, shuffle-clunked, back and forth. He shoved the full plate at her and retreated to the bathroom.

She stood in the middle of the kitchen holding the heaping plate of food and wondered what to do. Forgetting her prior instructions she timidly peeked her head into the dining room and headed for the table.

Immediately the big grandma swooped down on her and began a tirade in a mixture of broken English and Italian. Marie had not understood what she said but it made her mother cry as she steered her out to the back step.

"Mamma, why are you crying?"

"Oh, the old woman just said some unkind things, that's all. Marie, when we eat here you must eat on the back step, OK? That's a darling, just stay out here until I come for you."

Marie felt bad and confused as she ate on the step. She wondered about herself. What was so different about her than the other children in this large family? Was it because she was named Edna? Or was it because her hair was so blonde next to theirs? And why was the grandma so mean to Marie and so nice to Anginette? Anginette the fat grandma's darling—the cousin that wasn't really her cousin, which was all very confusing.

She decided then it must be because she wasn't pretty like Anginette with her big brown eyes and thick dark hair! That day she hadn't been able to make sense of anything, but she had decided that fat old woman was not her friend, or her mother's.

Even now, hanging socks in this dusty farmyard, just remembering that day made her feel bad. A few more years and some childish eavesdropping had made Marie understand that she and her mother were not considered part of that family. She smarted as she thought of the many times the old grandma had passed out presents to her darling grandchildren, *especially Anginette*, deliberately leaving Marie out.

Marie sniffed and wiped her eyes with the edge of a sock and thought about the last dinner they had with Giovanni's before moving. The fat grandma had been harsh with Marie again. After dinner the old man had come out to the back step, because he had not said much to her before she had been surprised.

"A—here child, I brought'a you some cookies, you like, no?" And he awkwardly pushed the plate of cookies toward Marie.

She was more than a little frightened of him and shrank away, all the time staring warily at him.

He bent over and slid the cookies into Edna Marie's lap and then with enormous effort, with little grunts and labored breathing, sat himself down on the step next to Marie.

"You—you like cookies, no?"

"Yes—s."

"Old'a grandmamma, she is good cook, no?"

Marie just stared at him over her cookie and nodded her head in agreement.

He grunted and kicked at a rock and awkwardly searching for English words, began again.

"Grandmamma—she, she so proud of her familia, we—come from the old'a country," all the while gesturing wildly with his hands, as though to better make her understand him.

"She—good'a Catholic, good'a mamma, to my bambinos, so. She proud of her Antonio, no?" He laboriously continued, lifting his shoulders and dipping his head in rhythm to his quaint way of speaking.

"She from the old'a country. We pick nice Italian girl for Antonio to marry, then—ah . . ."

He stared sadly down at his bony arthritic hands for some minutes . . . then continued, "He run off and marry your mamma. So, what can'a grandmamma do?

"She sound'a gruff to the little bambina—you. She no mean'a to be so gruff. She just cannot forget so easy that Antonio marry a Mormon. He cannot even marry this'a girl in the church, because she is ah—how you say—divorced.

"Ah, you must not mind old woman, she good'a mamma, just'a sad. So—eat'a your cookies little bambina . . ."

He sat with her in companionable silence for a few minutes, each thinking their own thoughts. As she munched on her cookie Marie pondered about the things he said.

Marie hadn't really understood much of his broken English but she heard him mention Mormons. Was that the reason the fat grandma hated Marie and her mother, because they were Mormons? She knew she was a Mormon, she knew it was a church, but she had only attended once in her life on the day she was confirmed. She didn't know another blessed thing about it. Was it bad to be a Mormon?

Before she could come to any satisfying conclusion, he had stood up and without even looking back at her, shuffled off muttering about all the trouble bambino's give to their mamma and papas.

As she hung clothes in the dusty farmyard she realized the kindness with which he had tried to explain the actions of his dread, enormous wife. Marie stomped her foot again and made another little dust cloud, but she didn't notice this one. She just didn't want the old man to be kind, not now, now that she had moved far away. She stomped her foot again, pursed her lips and shook her head.

"He probably did it just to make me cry," she shouted as she angrily swiped another tear from her dusty streaked face. "Well he won't!"

"Ed . . . na Marie, are you finished with those clothes yet?"

And for the second time that day Marie was jerked from her daydreams. She picked up the laundry basket and trudged toward the house.

Chapter Two

The screen door squeaked its protest as she pushed her basket of clothes through. Her eyes took in the sagging old kitchen in one disgusted sweep. How different it was from the bright sunny kitchen of her mother's first sweet home.

Marie's life here felt all topsy turvy too. Here in this old farmhouse in Walker she had been thrust back a half century or more in time.

At Grandpa Daddy's home, where she had lived until her mother got married again, they had always enjoyed the most modern innovations. As soon as some inventor had marketed his product, grandpa bought it. They had the first telephone in the town of Hiawatha—the first television too. She could remember sitting in the living room as a very tiny girl surrounded by neighbors who had come to watch the only T.V. in town.

A sudden longing to be held in Grandpa's arms tugged at Marie's heart, which was so quickly followed by her more familiar anger at him for leaving. Where was heaven? What was heaven? She only knew it was farther away than this town called Walker, and she could never see him again.

She stuffed the feelings deep inside as she set the clothes down on the nearest chair and looked around for her mother. Her mother had to work so hard stuffing the big black coal stove with wood, just to cook their meals and heat their water. Her one convenience was running water in the only sink in the house. They didn't even have a bathroom—imagine, you would think it was the turn of the century rather than 1960. She dreaded the thoughts of her mother stoking up that stove for dinner in the sweltering July heat.

In the next room Marie could hear drawers being closed as her mother put away the clean laundry she had just ironed and folded. She pushed open the door separating the kitchen from her mother's bedroom. The little farm house had no hallway just four small rooms, with doors leading directly from one into the other.

"Here's this batch of clothes, mamma; where should I set them?" Marie quietly asked her mother.

"Sssh, not so loud Edna Marie, you'll wake the boys."

Marie stood there feeling vexed. She didn't like that name, and she thought she had been quiet—and the look she gave her mother said so.

Ignoring Marie's look her mother impatiently said, "Here, set them here on the bed. I guess, it's as good a place as any in this room," and her eyes made a despairing sweep of things.

"Can I go read now, mamma?"

"Not yet dear. I really need to have you go to Hansen's Grocery first."

All the while she was thinking how tired her little girl looked and vowed to herself that Marie would not have to work so hard once the baby came.

But she kept her thoughts to herself and merely said, "Here now, I only have a little money. I need bread and a bar of soap."

Her mother turned and opened the top drawer in her dresser where she kept her money in an empty cigar box. She emptied it into her hand and counted only thirty-six cents.

"Now hurry so I can get dinner for your father on time, and if that isn't enough money tell Mr. Hansen we'll make up the difference next time." She thrust the money into Marie's grubby hand and began to iron the next shirt.

Marie took the money without a word and hurried out of the room. As she was leaving, she noticed her face in the mirror above her mother's second hand dresser. She wasn't certain which was worse, the scowl on her face or her tangled hair.

She went to her room to pull a brush through it, and thought, "Mamma always used to make me brush my hair in the mornings, now she doesn't even notice."

If her hair was somewhat improved, her bleak thoughts did nothing to improve her countenance as she headed for the front door. She shoved Patches off the porch and told him to "shoo." The cat landed in the dust. As he indignantly picked himself up he looked back reproachfully at his mistress.

Ignoring Marie's repentant calls of, "Kitty, Kitty—I'm sorry Patches," he ran into the nearest shed to continue his nap in peace.

Marie sighed and turned for the path to town. As she walked along the resentment in her heart threatened to spill over into more tears. She hated being called Edna again for what seemed like the tenth time that day. She'd been named Edna after her real father; Ed Rhinehart the man who had abandoned his wife and baby. Marie couldn't remember him at all, and she was glad. She just wished she didn't have to hear *his* name in her own, but more than that she hated having her mother call *that man* her father.

He wasn't her father. He was the little boys father and he was her mother's husband, but he wasn't her father! And it was his fault they moved to this horrible place. Oh why had her mother ever married him anyway? Marie had been so glad for her mother at first, when she seemed so happy, but then *he* lost his job at the coal mine and they started fighting. She wanted Grandpa Daddy for her father but he was dead!

In her agitation Marie stood still in the middle of the road and stomped her feet in the dust making a dust cloud sift into the sun. She watched it for a moment then sighed and headed down the road again, but she didn't relish going to the store again!

"Charity people, white trash, poor little thing," these were all words she'd heard grownups in town whisper whenever she or her mother went by. But they didn't whisper quietly enough; her hearing was good enough to hear their words and her feelings were raw enough to feel them as well.

So involved was Marie with her thoughts that she wasn't very mindful of where she was walking. She had been stomping down the dusty lane that led from their farmhouse into town for some time, when the next thing she knew she tripped over a twisted tree root sticking up near the road.

Before she could help herself she was face down on the edge of Stony Creek. She lay there for a minute trying to get her bearings while water trickled over her chin. She turned her head this way and that, while she wiggled her torso and legs to be certain she wasn't hurt.

With one hand in the water over the creek bank and the other hand on dry ground she began to hoist herself up, when she heard some muffled giggling behind her. There, not ten yards away, were two little boys, maybe five and seven years old, sitting on the bank of the creek swinging their bare legs and feet in the water. They grinned at her with delight and by the look on their face, she knew she had put on quite a show.

Just then a girl with shining, long hair the color of coal, and skin so fair she reminded Marie of "Snow White" walked up the road.

"You boys get on home, you know you shouldn't play down here by the crick—if you don't hurry I'll tell on you good."

The boys gave Marie one last grin as they scampered up the bank and raced each other for home.

"You must be from the new family that just moved into the old Benson farmhouse last month."

Marie looked up at this friendly, tall "Snow White" girl a little suspiciously, but timidly replied, "Y-es I am."

"Well, I'm Sharon Pace. Say I'll bet you're in at least the fifth grade aren't you?"

"No, I'm in the sixth grade," said Marie warming up to this exuberant, bright-eyed girl.

"Ooh, so am I. Did you know that we only have four people in the whole sixth grade—well five, now that you're here! Two boys and now three girls. That's super!

Did you come from a big city school with hundreds and hundreds of kids? We only have two classrooms for six grades here." Sharon exuberantly rattled on, hardly giving Marie the chance to answer her many questions.

"Well it wasn't a big city exactly but we did have at least twenty five kids in a classroom," Marie replied.

"We only have two teachers in our whole school. One teaches first, second and third grades and the other one teaches fourth, fifth and sixth—and she is the principal t'boot!"

Marie stared shyly at this happy girl for a moment and timidly asked where she lived.

"Oh I live clear over on the other side of town—there," as she pointed in the opposite direction from the farm.

"Say, tell ya what, ah . . . what did you say your name was?"

"Marie."

"Well Marie, can you play tomorrow?"

Without waiting for a reply she rushed on, "You meet me here at the same time and I'll show you where some nifty places are to play OK? I have to get home now; I'm supposed to be watching my little brothers. See you tomorrow."

And without waiting for an affirmative reply from Marie she skipped off across the big log bridge that lay across Stony Creek. She turned left at the fork road and Marie soon lost sight of her behind a haystack.

Marie stood in the road smiling for the longest time. Her bad mood had been swept away with a breath of friendly new air. She sat on the creek bank and bathed her skinned knees with cool creek water, hardly believing the joy and hope that sprang up in her young heart!

She stood up, flicked the water off her hands toward the heavens and did a graceful pirouette right there in the road. With a lightheartedness she hadn't felt in a long time she hastened off to Hansen's store.

The bell tinkled as Marie pushed open the door. She went directly to the bread counter and began trying to find the cheapest loaf. After checking everything at least seven times she reached up and pulled a loaf from the shelf, it cost twenty six cents.

Her heart was afraid as she headed for the soap isle. What would she do if a bar of soap cost more than she had? She began to feel extremely pessimistic again. She just knew it would be more.

How she hated to beg. She'd already done it enough in this very store! Resentment for all the times she had been made to shop without enough money began to build in her. She tried not to blame her mother. She knew her family went without so many things lately and when there was just no other choice, like today when there was not a sliver of soap in the house and hadn't been for four days and not a crust of bread, she just had to go to Hansen's store.

Marie looked at every bar of soap on the shelf. Dial, Zest, Brand X. They all cost more than eleven cents. She stood in the isle checking them, again and again, hoping somehow that one would magically read eleven cents. Finally she stopped looking and took down a bar of Brand X, trying to muster the courage to ask Mr. Hansen if he could let her pay him the difference next time.

Her reluctant heart said, "What about last time?" But she'd have to say next time, again.

While she stood there Mr. Hansen walked over and put his hand on her shoulder. Startled, she jumped back and looked up at the kind, gray haired old man.

"Can I help you with something, Marie?"

"Oh, I—I, just needed some bread," she waved her loaf at him, "and a bar of soap, sir." Then she held up her other hand showing him Brand X.

"Well, young lady," he smiled, "I guess you found them all rightey then, come on over and let's ring em'up."

She followed him to the check out counter with her head down in shame, all the while rehearsing her begging speech.

She plopped the bread and soap up on the counter and looked up briefly at Mr. Hansen. He looked down just in time to see a tear slide down her face.

"What's the matter Marie, don't you have enough money to pay for these again?"

She just looked at the floor and shook her dejected head.

"Well, I guess your mamma needs these pretty bad, doesn't she?"

Marie, still looking at the floor, nodded her head up and down this time.

"You know, Marie, you never need more than a few extra nickels or pennies, and I'm happy to wait until things are better—until you can pay. I don't mind," he said. As he looked down at her silent misery, an idea formed quickly in his mind.

"Tell you what Marie, can you sweep a floor?"

That got her attention and she looked up at him in surprise.

"U-huh," she nodded.

"Well this floor get's mighty dusty every day, yep, mighty dusty. Tell you what—whenever you need something and your mamma doesn't have quite enough money, you come on over to my store anyway.

You get what you need, and before you leave you can sweep my floor. Then we're square Marie, you won't owe me a cent. Now chipper up lass, how does that sound?"

Marie looked up at old Mr. Hansen and suddenly his white hair, mustache and twinkley eyes made him look just like an angel. Her gratitude spilled over into a big grin, and her eyes said it all. He rang up her purchase, bagged it and pushed it aside, handing her a broom. She smiled at him again and began to sweep.

This kind, gentle man, he understood—he really understood! With her heart swelling with joy for the second time that day, Marie attacked that floor with gusto! She had never swept a floor so well in her life. She returned to the counter with the broom and timidly asked:

"Where is the broom closet? I can put this away for you."

"Well, Marie, have you finished?"

Mr. Hansen surveyed the room, "You did a fine job, yep, so fine I believe I now owe you," and with that he reached up for the candy jar. He lifted it down to her level and offered her a piece.

Chapter Three

Marie woke up with a start. She sat up in bed and wondered for a moment where she was. Then it all came back to her mind, she was in the old farmhouse in Walker. She eased herself carefully back down in bed for fear she would wake her little brother.

Little Tony slept with Marie in a rickety trundle bed, on the side that could be pushed down and under her twin side of the bed. He also slept on the side that was broken, so Marie lay very still on her side of the bed and watched the sunrise begin to lighten the tiny window high in the corner of her bedroom.

She heard farmer Adams' rooster crow in the distance and wondered for a moment why she felt glad this day had begun. Suddenly she remembered—Sharon!

Today she would meet her in the glen by the creek. Forgetting all caution, she popped out of bed.

Snap!

"Mamma, mamma, awaaaaaah!"

Oh that bed! Marie had bumped the trundle side ever so slightly and it had bucked little Tony onto the floor. Marie's mother came stumbling into the room.

"Tony, what's the matter honey?" Marie's mother picked up the crying boy from the floor as she shot her nearly twelve-year old an exasperated look.

"Marie, can't you be more careful? You know that bed scares little Tony to death when it falls. I've told you and told you to be more careful!

Come on Tony, you can sleep in my bed for awhile." She scooped him up and carried him to her room, muttering all the while, "Now I'll never get him to sleep in his bed. If it's not one thing it's another, I can't sleep, I just can't sleep."

Marie sank dejectedly onto the corner of the bed. Her lip trembled a bit and she wondered why she was so careless; how she hated to have her mother unhappy with her. She couldn't help remembering when she was the only child her mother had.

Maybe it was those babies that had changed her mother. She always used to smile at Marie as she read to her, took her to the park and sang to her. Now all she did was make her work, while telling her how clumsy and slow she was.

Marie wrapped her arms around her knees and rolled her body back into bed. As she climbed into it's warmth she lay there thinking—in her heart she knew the babies weren't the problem. The problem now, of course, must be that she was no longer an adorable baby. Marie was almost twelve years old—nearly an adult.

Last month she had tried to climb into her mother's lap and when she didn't fit Emma had pushed her off and said, "Oh Marie, get off, you're much too big to sit on my lap—you're nearly twelve years old.

"You can't sit on my lap anymore, especially with the baby coming. Run along now," and with that her mother lumbered into the other room.

The look on her mother's face as she commented on

Marie's size hadn't been a look of adoration. Marie couldn't read her mind of course, so she decided that her mother wasn't very pleased with her new size.

She climbed out of bed again and ran over to the cracked mirror above her dresser. Marie loved the little mirror. She had found it out in one of the old sheds and begged her mother to let her bring it to her room. Even though it was cracked, it was (or used to be) very beautiful.

The frame was warped and cracked now, but Marie could tell that it had been painted white with a tiny gold trim which curled and curved in the loveliest way. The day Marie hung it on her wall it conjured up such a vision for her. In her minds eye it transformed that drab little room into a bedroom fit for a princess.

The high small window had become large, with a cushioned love seat just below. The windows had beautiful white panes and when Marie sat at the seat and pushed the window open, she could see into a magic garden filled with shrubs and trees and flowers. A gentle breeze wafted through the window and brushing past the cherry tree in bloom, brought with it a lovely scent to fill the air.

Turning from the window, Marie could open her spacious closet to choose from among her many pretty dresses. High up on one wall hung a shelf with curlicue brackets of white and gold that faithfully held their burden of wonderful, gorgeous dolls. There was a china face doll, a bride doll, a fashion doll, a pretty little pink baby doll, large dolls and small, and of course her ballerina doll.

A shadow of gloom suddenly engulfed Marie as she though about her ballerina doll, but on this day of promise she simply refused to entertain the miserable thoughts. *Instead she giggled to see her ballerina on that shelf of marvelous dolls, for Ballerina was rather tattered. Her hair was matted and the fingers on her right hand were chewed off, but that was OK.* She would have her place on the shelf, because Marie loved her dearly anyway, and she would never never forget her.

As her eye moved away from the shelf of wonderful dolls, she could see her petite dresser. With the mirror hanging above it; it stood properly and gracefully holding its bottles of perfume, a vase of flowers, and a breathtaking picture of—herself.

She was dressed in white and sat among flowers. The photographer had captured her curly, golden-blonde hair sparkling in the sun. Of course the tilt of her chin and the angle of her nose was perfect as she gazed serenely at her bouquet of pink rosebuds.

On the other side of the room was the white canopy bed, with a sheer pink bedspread made with three layers of ruffles and lace. At the foot of the bed stood her white and gold hope chest.

Once she had seen a picture in a magazine of a room just like this one and she had asked her mother about the chest. She told her it was a hope chest, into which, rich girls placed all the lovely things they were saving for a home of their own some day.

Well, that was swell. That is just what Marie did. Whenever she just couldn't stand her present world, in her minds eye Marie would lift the lid of her magic chest and hope. She always had the key tucked away in her heart.

"Ma-rie, Marie, are you up? I need help with breakfast so get dressed quickly!"

Her mother always managed to splash cold water on her best daydreams!

"Coming mamma, be there in a minute."

Marie looked into the dusty cracked mirror again. She looked long and hard for a moment at her freckled face. It had definitely lost that adorable baby look. Her nose was growing faster than the rest of it. Her golden blonde hair was so tangled it made her think of a very funny young witch.

As she stuck her tongue out, she noticed that at least her teeth had grown back, but they came in much too large for her mouth. Her mother said not to worry, that when she grew up everything would be in the proper order, but Marie just wasn't sure.

She grabbed her brush and started to yank the snarls out of her hair. She screwed up her face, wrinkled her freckled nose and stuck out her tongue at the strange girl in the cracked mirror again.

She decided her mom wasn't as nice to her, because she must not like big girls; her mom only liked chubby little babies. Well, Marie couldn't be a chubby little baby anymore so as she got dressed and went into the kitchen to help, she determined again that she would make up for it by being good.

Maybe, just maybe if she tried very hard to obey her mother and help her she would feel the way she used to feel about her. Marie squared her shoulders and went into the kitchen with a smile.

"Hi mamma, isn't it a beautiful day?"

"No, it's hot already. Hand me the large bowl, Marie, and then go out to the woodpile and fetch more wood."

Marie shrugged her shoulders and did as she was told. She did as she was told all morning. After feeding her little brothers lunch she got them down for naps.

Then her mother said, “Marie, we still have more laundry to fold and the kitchen needs to be cleaned up. I’m so tired, I’m going to lie down for awhile. Could you be a dear and get started on it?”

Marie hesitated before she spoke. She wanted so badly to go meet Sharon, yet she wanted to please her mother. How good, she wondered, was good enough, until her mother adored her again?

“Mamma, I—I met a new girl yesterday, down by the bridge.”

“That’s nice dear; don’t forget to wipe off the counter.”

“Mamma, she was really nice and she’s in my grade at school!” Marie hurried to say.

“Yes, well I’m going in my room now.”

Before Marie could say another word the door closed firmly in her face. She stood with the door nearly touching her nose for a minute, then lifted her fist to knock. Instead her hand slowly dropped to her side; she sighed as she turned to the table, picked up some dishes, and carried them to the sink.

She paused to look up at the small window and noticed a bird sitting still on a limb. Out of the corner of her eye, as Marie turned to go back to the table, she saw the bird lift his wings and take flight. On an impulse she brushed past the table and headed purposefully toward that closed door. Squaring her shoulder’s, she took a deep breath, raised her fist again, and knocked.

“Marie,” came her mother’s sleepy voice, “What is it? I’m trying to sleep.”

“Mom, the new girl, Sharon’s her name, she asked me to play today. Can I go now? I’ll help later I promise—please?”

"Oh, I don't know, I need your help . . ."

"Please, mom, please?"

Marie's mother lay there in the shadows of her darkened bedroom and looked at the eager face of her daughter. She felt another pang of guilt and a deep sense of despair. As she rolled her swollen body over, she quietly mumbled, "OK."

Marie wasn't sure she heard her right and blurted, "Did you say I can go?"

Irritated now, she raised her voice and gruffly said, "Go—go now before I change my mind!"

"Oh, thanks mamma, gosh thanks!" And Marie bolted for the door before her mother could change her mind.

Marie skipped and hop-glided down the dusty lane, hoping all the while Sharon would show up, until she skidded to a neat stop at the creek bank and surveyed the area. Not a sign of Sharon. Maybe she changed her mind, maybe her mom wouldn't let her come, maybe . . .

"Maybe a bee'll land in your hair
He wouldn't dare
Maybe a ghost'll give you a scare
He wouldn't dare
Maybe you'll trip and fall off your chair
I wouldn't dare."

Marie loved to play word games. Sometimes, when she was worried or scared, she'd make up silly dittys to take her mind off her problems. She sat on the log bridge that lay across Stony Creek swinging her legs and chanting,

"Or in your dress you'll get a tear

I don't care
Maybe she didn't like your hair
I don't care."

"I DON'T CARE!" Marie shouted and jumped off the bridge onto the bank.

She ran along the creek a short distance to a spot she had leveled for a stage last week, and lost herself in the willows and weeds. They were taller than Marie and she felt perfectly secluded and safe.

There she began to twirl and dip and curtsy to an imaginary audience cheering her on. As the applause grew so did her enthusiasm and confidence. She leaped and cavorted and bowed again and again. Finally she bowed a last curtsy and sank to the ground out of breath.

"Again, do it again!"

Marie spun around to find a delighted Sharon clapping and grinning at her.

"Ah, you came, you—where did you come from?" Marie said this as her face burned red with embarrassment.

"Yes, I told you I would. I came and you weren't there so I waited on the bridge for awhile. Then I heard this sort of thrashing noise in the willows—so I came to look," she said with a delighted teasing chuckle.

Marie just stood there looking embarrassed.

"Don't worry Marie, I thought you were wonderful. Where did you learn to dance like that anyway?"

"Oh, I don't really know how to dance. I've never had lessons. Well, not real ones anyway."

"What do you mean, not real ones?"

"Well, see—my cousins had lessons and I could go watch them, but I wasn't in their class so I just watched," said Marie, hoping Sharon would understand.

"Why didn't you have lessons too?"

Marie hated that question, so she hesitated and studied Sharon for a time.

Impatiently Sharon prodded, "So why Marie? Why didn't you have lessons too? Was the class too big?"

Marie knew this was a good out; she could just agree and change the subject or tell Sharon the real reason. She looked at her tattered shoes and then back at Sharon's eyes.

She knew she wouldn't really be fooling Sharon so she said, "We didn't have the money."

"Oh," was all Sharon said, innocently unconcerned—then added, "but you dance like you've had lessons all your life. You looked like a fairy princess twirling in the willows."

Marie giggled and knew she really liked this girl.

"Sharon, do you like romantic books about far away places?"

"Oh yes," cried Sharon, "and I love fairy tales the best. I love how they always end happy. Do you read too, Marie?"

Marie curtsied, did a pirouette and ended in a dramatic stance.

Laughing, she said, "You wouldn't know it but this dancing fairy princess doesn't turn into a frog, or a toad, or a bird, but I turn into a worm, every time I get a free moment!"

"A book worm of course," said Sharon teasingly.

"Well, I have to tell you that I may be a bookworm, but I don't like fairy tales."

"Why not?"

"Because they aren't real, they're dumb. Life isn't like

that! Bad things happen all the time and it never turns out so nice. Nobody ever really lives happily ever after!"

"That's not true, lots of people live happy lives."

"Well, plenty of people live awful ones too."

Sharon, who was a basically happy, beloved child, in spite of her mother's restrictions, couldn't really understand Marie's attitude. And she could see that she wasn't going to change her mind about fairy tales anytime soon, so she changed the subject.

"So, what else do you like to do?"

"I like to climb trees; don't you just love them too, Sharon?"

"Trees?" Sharon said with derision. "Boys climb trees."

"Well, have you ever tried it?"

"No, my mother would kill me."

"Oh, that's too bad," Marie said with disappointment. She was never going to suggest that anyone disobey their mother.

But although Sharon was a good girl, she didn't quite have Marie's sense of obedience. It stemmed mainly from her mother, who was a very forceful person. She could make her obey through loss of privileges or other threats, but Sharon was a child of understanding and she intuitively knew that her mother was often unfair and wrong in her assumptions. And so, even though she was a little frightened of her mother's wrath, this only made her more determined to do what she wanted when she could sneak in the chance.

So although she wasn't very interested in the idea of climbing a tree, the chance to do something she knew her mother wouldn't approve of began to intrigue her.

"Marie, what's it like—I mean—why do you do it?

You don't seem like the tomboy type."

"I certainly am not a TOMBOY, but I don't let people push me around either. I don't do something just because it's for boys or girls. I do things because I like to."

"OK, but why do you like to?"

"Because, Sharon, trees are wonderful. They cool you when it's hot. You can hide in them and be almost invisible. I love to climb a nice big friendly tree and sit in a 'just right crook' and read!"

"What's a 'just right crook'?"

"Well, it's hard to explain," said Marie, "like it's hard to explain that trees are wonderful. Do you know they can whisper to you?"

"What? Trees can't talk," said Sharon. She was beginning to think this girl was nuts.

"Oh, I know that! Just use your imagination Sharon. I didn't say they talk, I said they whisper. They have personalities too, you know."

"Oh Marie, trees don't whisper and they aren't like people." Sharon laughed and continued, "You are an unusual girl Marie—but I like you." She said with a smile!

Marie smiled back but wouldn't drop the subject. "Sharon, it's true about trees you know."

"Marie, how do you know?"

"Well, you said yourself you never climb 'em, right?"

"Yeah, so?"

"So, I have. I've climbed all kinds of trees. Cottonwood trees, pine trees, oak trees, and lots of other trees I don't even know the names of. So, Sharon, I can't explain this to you if you haven't climbed them yourself. I guess you'll just have to take my word for it."

"Oh Marie," laughed Sharon, "I can't believe it, but

you make me want to climb a tree!"

She grabbed Marie's hand and began dragging her out of the willows. "Marie, come on, let's go climb a tree, right now. Maybe it will whisper to me."

Marie held back and looked concerned as she said, "Sharon, no. You said your mom would kill you. Let's not."

"Marie," she stopped and put her hands on her hips, "I said my mom would kill me if she found out about it. I didn't say I would never do it."

"Yes, but just the same, don't you feel bad about disobeying your mother?"

"Well, for goodness sake, Marie, I wouldn't do anything really terrible. You act like I'm not a nice girl or something."

"I'm sorry Sharon, that's not what I meant."

"So what's the big deal?"

Marie had such a sense of right and wrong and she felt that she could never disobey her mother, but, her mother had never told her not to climb a tree—thank heavens.

So she said, "Come on then, there's a great one around the bend."

They scrambled down the bank and walked around the bend by the creek. There, looming over the creek, was an enormous, wonderful tree. It's limbs started growing low with great wide angles that made it easy to climb.

At first Sharon was timid, but Marie showed such confidence and expertise, that Sharon soon scuttled up the tree with just as much grace. They stopped at the spot Marie loved and were still for a long moment.

Then Sharon, with almost reverent wonder said, "Marie I hear it, it's whispering—just like you said."

They sat enraptured for awhile until Marie said, "Sharon I've always wanted to build a tree house."

"A tree house, now wait, that's too . . ."

Marie cut her off, "Too what—too tomboy?"

"Well," Sharon said hesitatingly, "what kind of tree house?"

"Just a simple one, one that you could disguise somehow."

"How would you do that?"

"I haven't really thought it out, all the way yet." Marie said as her eyes scanned the creek banks searchingly.

Suddenly focusing her eyes on the other side of the creek she exclaimed, "Sharon, look at that rock!"

"So, it's a rock."

"So, look at it more carefully."

Sharon strained her eyes and leaned a little on the limb of the tree. "Where Marie?"

"There," pointed Marie, "See the crack in the . . ."

She heard a snapping noise and turned just in time to see Sharon disappear.

"Sharon!" Screamed Marie as she scuttled out of the tree and found Sharon sitting waist deep on the bottom of the creek.

Sharon looked up at Marie with surprise. They stared at each other for a second and then both broke out in laughter, as Marie put out her arm and hauled the wet Sharon out of the water.

They sat on the edge of the creek and giggled. They rolled on the grass and laughed until their sides hurt.

"Maaa-rie! Ed-na Maa-ri-ee!"

"Sharon, that's my mom calling."

"Oh, too bad, Marie; this was just so much fun today.

Can we play again?"

"Yes, of course, tomorrow?"

"No, my cousins are coming from Newcastle tomorrow. I have to stay home and entertain them," Sharon said regretfully.

"Maybe you could bring them here."

"No, I better not do that."

"OK, but how will I know when you can play again?"

"Well silly, I'll just call you on the phone."

"We—" Marie looked down at her shoes as she spoke, "we don't have a phone."

"Oh," Sharon seemed surprised but didn't question Marie.

Marie noticed Sharon's wet clothes and said, "What are you going to tell your mother Sharon?"

"That I fell in the creek, silly. Did you want me to lie to her?" And she grinned at Marie.

"NO, of course not."

"Look Marie," said Sharon as she dragged her to the middle of the log bridge. "See that big red barn way over there," and she pointed to the other side of town.

"Yes," said Marie squinting her eyes hard, "just barely."

"Well, when I want you to come to the creek, I'll hang a white flag on the flagpole on top of our barn."

"That sounds like something out of *Anne of Green Gables*."

"That's where I got the idea. Can you see it?"

"I hope so."

"Don't worry, you can. That's how I used to signal my big brother to come home for lunch when he worked for Brother Adams. That was almost as far away as this.

So watch for my signal next week, OK? We'll meet here at the same time." With that she waved and ran across the bridge toward home.

"Ma-rie, Ed-na Ma-riee!" She could hear her mother's voice rising with irritation, so she turned in the opposite direction and ran down the dusty lane for home.

Chapter Four

Marie watched for the signal every day the next week. Just to be certain she hadn't missed Sharon, every afternoon she'd wander down by the creek.

"Why didn't she come back?" Marie wondered, "Was I too eager to play? Didn't she like me? Maybe she didn't think I was very pretty. Maybe her cousins are still there?"

Marie had nearly given up hope of having Sharon for a friend, but—she would tell herself, "we had such a good time. I liked her and she liked me. I know she did!" And so her thoughts would waver between fear and hope.

If she still hoped that she had found a true friend in this town, her hope that things would improve at home was growing dimmer. Marie's only escape was between the pages of books.

She never did enjoy a book as much the second time and she only owned a few; her favorite was *The Secret Garden.* A week after meeting Sharon she was in the tree again, trying to read *The Secret Garden* for the third time.

This time when her mother called, Marie was grateful to go to Hansen's store. After she finished sweeping for Mr. Hansen she mustered the courage to ask him if the town had a library.

"Well, my dear," he said thoughtfully, scratching his head, "that's somethin' this here town's never had. No, the folks here have to drive to Newcastle for that."

Then he glanced down as he handed Marie her piece of candy for the day's sweeping. He sensed her disappointment and it tugged at his kind heart, until he remembered something.

"Course," he said with a twinkle in his eye, "there is the school library. Why, we just aren't even used to having a school in our little village here. Wouldn't have a library if Mrs. Jemison hadn't bought near every book in it. No sir, we wouldn't even have a school if'n it weren't for Mrs. Jemison."

Nearly forgetting who he was speaking to, Mr. Hansen glanced down at the young girl waiting patiently to make sense of his ramblings.

He smiled broadly at her and said, "Yep, that new school across the street does have a library in it."

"Mr. Hansen," Marie said in a perplexed voice, "how come you didn't have a school?"

"Well, my dear—if'n a person was to sneeze while passin' this town he'd be just as likely to miss it as not. We're jest farmers out here lass. Even I farmed all my life.

"So the school board didn't see the necessity of givin' a town this size a school, but they didn't reckon with the likes of Mrs. Jemison. She and just about every other parent in town fought hard to have a school.

"Yes sir. We might just be farmer's, but our kids need a good school—a good one close to home."

He smiled at Marie and kept rambling. "I jest farmed all my life, but it's a good life—farming!"

"But, if you're a farmer, what about your store?"

"Oh shucks, this was my dear departed wife's project. She just got so fed up with drivin' fifty miles to the nearest grocery, she done started her own. It brought in a little extree cash and—it made all the ladies in town mighty happy."

As his eyes filled with tears for a brief moment, he looked deeply into Marie's and said, "Marie, I never knew then what a blessing it would be to me too. My old bones can't farm anymore 'n all my kids moved off to the city. They wanted me to come, . . ." he stared off thoughtfully and nearly forgot he was speaking to Marie.

Then he shook himself and smiled again as he continued, "But, I have my store. I'm mighty grateful to Arlene, bless her soul. So here I stay and here I die. Would anyway if'n those kids carted me off to that noisy Salty Lake of a City!"

And with that, he started off into the back room.

Marie watched him depart and headed for the door. She sighed her disappointment as she wondered what good the library in the school would do, until school started. Just as she opened the door to leave, Mr. Hansen came bustling out of the back room chuckling and clucking to himself.

"Marie—here, hold on a minute girl. I fergot what we was a talkin' 'bout. I reckon you could talk to Mrs. Jemison 'n see if you could loan a book or two b'fore school starts."

Surprised, Marie turned around and asked, "Who's Mrs. Jemison?"

"Why, she's the school principal—lives just next door here."

Just then a tall, noisy lady bustled into the store. Her manner suggested she must be very busy. As she said good day to Mr. Hansen Marie could see that she talked very fast and crisp, but with a happy sort of bird-like lilt to her voice too.

In fact, thought Marie, this lady seemed sort of bird like. Not a little sparrow type, but big and capable—all arms and legs with knees and elbows protruding like knobs on a bedpost.

She had a large hooked nose that would be wonderful on a witch, but you could never mistake this lady for a witch! Witches did not have big, toothy smiles that twinkled all the way to their eyes like hers did.

Mr. Hansen grinned and greeted her with happy delight, introducing Marie.

"Marie, this here's Mrs. Jemison, the school marm I was tellin' you 'bout." He said this as though he were infinitely proud of himself for having brought the two together.

"Mrs. Jemison, this here's a new student for your school. Considerin' the size of it I know you'll be down right dee-lighted!"

"Hi, Marie," Mrs. Jemison said in her quick, happy way. "So Mr. Hansen's told you about the school marm next door has he? And what has he been saying?"

The kindness and friendly jesting of these good people amazed and warmed Marie. She had never experienced anything like it in her life before. She was not sophisticated enough to think of a clever reply, but their mood was catching.

She could not help grinning from ear to ear as she simply said, "He just said you were the school principal and that your new school has a library in it."

"A library now, it does at that. And what interest might you have in a library?"

Marie's grin spread from her mouth to her eyes as she gushed almost with reverence, "Oh, I love to read!"

"Ah, I see that lass, indeed I do. So I'll bet it might be of interest to you to see that library before school will be starting—am I right?"

And she smiled in the most beautiful, charming way for a woman with such misshapen features, that it was like looking into a very poorly wrapped present to find the most priceless and beautiful gift inside.

"Oh, yes ma'am, could I?"

"For certain, and my shopping can wait. Can you come now?"

Wild horses could not have kept Marie from going then. She followed Mrs. Jemison across the street to the little red brick school house; it was an intriguing building. Mrs. Jemison could not help but notice Marie's interest and so she treated her to a grand tour.

"As you heard Mr. Hansen say, the school is only two years old. We only have two class rooms, one for the first, second and third grades, and one for the fourth, fifth and sixth grades."

Her happy chirping voice went on to explain that she had fought the school board for many years to win the privilege of having a building in their small town. She explained how her own small children had to be bussed to Newcastle, nearly fifty miles away, to attend school.

Marie only half listened as she stared at the little school. Inside the front door was a straight and narrow hallway ending with a glass door at the back through which she could see the playground. There were two doors spaced almost exactly apart on both sides of the hallway, making four doors in all. Mrs. Jemison unlocked one and they went inside.

The classroom had less than twenty desks, but

otherwise looked exactly like every other school Marie had attended, except for the folding door down the middle of the room. Mrs. Jemison explained as she unfolded it that it combined the two classes.

In the winter when the weather was bad they would push all the desks against the wall and have gym together in this room. "How wonderful," thought Marie.

Back out in the hall and across from the classroom doors she noticed the same type of folding doors in a sort of window. Mrs. Jemison opened another door and took her into the kitchen. There the cook prepared hot lunch, which she would pass through the window into the hall for the children when it was lunchtime. They would then take their trays back to their desk to eat.

"How very strange," thought Marie, as they entered the other door on the left side of the lunch window. Inside and just behind the door was a teacher's desk.

"This is the principal's office," said Mrs. Jemison, pointing to the desk.

"And this is the library," she explained as her arm swept the rest of the room.

On three walls of the large room were shelves—shelves with wonderful and very new books on them. Mrs. Jemison watched the child as she walked over to the rows of books and touched them almost reverently.

For the first time she noticed how grubby her hand was and how tattered her clothes were. In that moment Mrs. Jemison determined to love and help this child, who obviously shared her love of reading.

Marie joyfully took an armful of books home to read in her apple tree. She was learning to love it almost as much as the dear old oak in her old home, except that it had stickers instead of sweet clean grass beneath it and it wasn't quite as comfortable.

To increase her tree's comfort and to help fill the long lonely days, she made herself a very simple tree house. It consisted of three planks of wood nailed together with the help of a large rock and some rusty bent nails. She placed it in a good crook high up in the apple tree.

The planks of wood were different lengths and, not having a saw to cut them with nor the experience or strength to do it if she had one, she had to nail them together as they were. The ragged ends of her tree house irritated Marie. They seemed unfinished and shabby, so she faced them toward the farmhouse and never looked that way at all. Instead, whenever she was in her treehouse, she faced toward the field across the street.

Another hot day six weeks later found Marie in the apple tree again after a trying morning of tending babies. A gentle welcoming breeze ruffled her blonde hair, which she had thoroughly brushed that morning. She lay on her back munching a big green apple, while trying to decide which school library book to read again.

She had read all ten books which were piled high on the longest plank of her treehouse. She looked at them and mentally tried to thumb through each one, but thoughts of Sharon kept getting in the way.

"Why do I keep having such bad luck?" she said to Patches who had joined her, nearly knocking her books off to settle next to Marie.

Glad for her company, Marie stroked her cat's long tangled fur as she poured out her heart to the sounds of contented purring.

"Why doesn't Sharon like me? Nobody in this town

likes me Kitty. Sometimes when I'm there I hear people whisper things about me and it makes me feel bad. Now just look at you, you have an easy life! You have plenty of fat mice to eat in the sheds and you have me to love you."

Patches looked up and gave Marie a little meow, as if to say it's not always perfect for me, either. Marie laughed and agreed that Patches did have a hard time dodging the little boys.

Just yesterday Bradley tearfully handed Marie a handful of grey and yellow fur as he showed her the Kitty scratches on his arm that needed a kiss.

Patches meowed again and began licking Marie's bare toes as though to say, "I love you too."

The cat's affection reminded Marie that it wasn't quite true that everyone in town hated her.

Some of the people here were nicer than any other people she had ever known! She smiled happily to herself as she thought of each of them in turn. Good Mr. Hansen, her first friend in this strange town; he let her sweep his store because he understood—and he even gave her candy!

Then of course Sharon—a shadow suddenly passed over the tree and Marie looked up to see a big cloud slowly drift by; it seemed to bring with it the feeling of a bad omen. But just as quickly as it came, the cloud moved on and the sun popped back out.

Just so were Marie's feelings. She decided to quit worrying about why Sharon didn't come back to play. They had liked each other so very much and had such a great time together, Marie trusted her. Sharon must have had a good reason for not coming.

Finishing her apple she tossed it aside and rolled onto her tummy. Peeking through her window of leaves she could see far off the main highway. Mostly trucks and semi-trucks passed on the lonely country road, with a few cars in between which looked like toys from here. Her gaze followed a hay wagon slowly bumping along into town.

"I'm going into town myself on Monday morning," she thought, "for the first day of school."

The green apples she had just eaten combined with the thoughts of a new school made her tummy do flip-flops.

Marie glanced over at Patches who was just finishing his bath. He cautiously clawed his way down the tree; at the bottom he looked up at Marie with a meow for good-bye and trotted off for the sheds.

"I'll be saying goodbye to you soon too, Kitty," thought Marie.

She turned back to her window of leaves and looked beyond the highway to the golden wheat fields gently moving with the hot summer breeze. The undulating wheat seemed to beckon her, soothing her fears and calling up the image of the cheery big bird lady, who would be her teacher.

Chapter Five

Marie rushed out of the house and down the lane with her heart pounding. Then remembering her hair, she slowed down and patted it gently with her hand, wishing she had a barrette. Well, it probably wouldn't help anyway, and she was grateful that today it was at least clean.

Just last night she had lugged the old tub into the kitchen and poured pan after pan of hot water from the wood stove into it. For once her mother let her be the first one in the tub. How wonderful it was to slip into clean hot water and soak again. Since moving here she hadn't bathed in clean water. The babies always had to use it first—ick!

At the bridge Marie stopped, realizing school didn't start for some time. Marie was always on time. In fact she was always early for everything, especially school. She hated making an entrance with everyone staring at her. She would rather stay home than go late. She always tried to be early so she could pick out an inconspicuous place to observe everyone else who was arriving. People didn't notice you as much and it felt a lot safer.

Stopping at the bridge, Marie suddenly realized she didn't know the rules at this school. Some schools let you go inside right away. If this one did, then she would go to her desk and have a few wonderful minutes to read her latest book.

Marie always carried a book with her. Once she had a teacher who let her miss recess to read right at her desk. Usually they made her go outside, saying she needed to socialize and get fresh air. She didn't even know which desk was hers at this school.

She stood by the bridge and breathed in great gulps of wonderful morning air. It was just as warm as any other summer day, but with an autumn difference somehow. Marie was as excited for school to start, as she was terrified.

"What if the kids don't like me? What if Mrs. Jemison doesn't? I think Mrs. Jemison likes me fine—and Patches, you go on home!"

She realized she had been stroking his patchwork fur and talking to him.

"How did you get here? You followed me, didn't you kitty, shoo. Go home!" Marie mumbled down the lane, "Just what I need, to start my first day of school in a new town, like *Mary*—who *Had a Little Lamb*."

She already knew the walk well, because she had been to the school library several times in the last few weeks. Down the lane past the bridge, around the sharp corner, then past the side street with the first few town houses and you were on main street.

Main street scared her because it was a state highway. The large semi-trucks that passed through town so frequently hardly ever slowed down as they should. Once she was nearly run over by one, after a shopping trip for her mom.

She stopped before going across the highway. On her right was the church, on her left Mr. Hansen's store, and across the street was the school.

She could see that she must be the very first child at school that day. For a moment she wondered if she had the right day; how silly she would feel if not.

After waiting for a pickup truck loaded with rowdy boys shoving and teasing and nearly spilling out the back, right in front of the school, she knew she had the right day. How she disliked rowdy boys—mean, loud, pushy, rowdy boys!

"Oh darn," she lamented, "I waited too long at the bridge."

She scuffed her shoe on the gravely road in disgust, and with a sigh she squared her shoulders and quickly crossed the highway. On the other side she lowered her eyes and tried to rush into the school yard past the boys.

"Hey," said one of the boys, "who's that?"

"Don't you know?" asked another. "That's the poor kid; lives in the old farm house outsida' town. And you know what, she ain't even a Mormon. Her dad smokes!"

"Well that's a switch," thought Marie. "First the old grandma doesn't like me because I am a Mormon and now these boys don't like me because they think I'm not!" It was getting harder all the time to understand this Mormon stuff.

"She ain't comin' to school here is she?"

Marie dived through the crowd of boys and emerged at the front door, which was locked.

Locked! Now what? She just stood staring at that locked front door, wanting to disappear, willing it to open. Just as she heard one taunting boy approaching her, the door opened—in Marie fell.

From the floor she saw Mrs. Jemison's shoes. Slowly she looked up and there was Mrs. Jemison, grinning from ear to ear.

"Well now, if it isn't my new student."

Marie grinned sheepishly up at her from the floor. Then, picking herself up, she apologized.

"No problem, dear. Why don't you come in and give me a hand for a moment? Will you put one of these books on each desk?"

As Marie went inside, she could hear the delighted guffaws grow suddenly dim as they huddled to whisper. It was almost worse than the loud laughter and jeering remarks. She could only imagine what they were saying now.

"Her dad smokes."

"Yeah, and my mom said she'd wallop me and my sister if we ever go near her place."

"We ain't allowed to play with her, neither, cause she ain't even a Mormon!"

"She is too! I heard she was baptized same as me and you. Only she ain't ever been to church!"

"Huh, that's worse than not being Mormon. She's a Jack Mormon."

"Well I'm not allowed to play with her no matter what she is."

"I wouldn't want to anyhow. She's just a dumb girl."

"And my Pa says anyone'd live in that old place—can't amount to much good."

"Looks haunted, don't it?"

"Looks like her—she's an ugly Klutz!" Which remark brought forth a volley of knee slapping convulsions that lasted until the bell rang.

And that was how Marie acquired her first ugly nickname, from the leader of the gang, Jack Carlson.

In the coming weeks and months, Jack Carlson would do anything he could to make her life miserable. He always had to be the center of attention. He thought he was really funny—really something! And making fun of Marie always gave him center stage.

"Flees, Stinky, Turkey Legs, Jack Mormon" (whatever that was), and "EDNA" (because he knew it made her so mad) were all names Jack taught the boys to call her when they spoke to her and mostly about her, in the coming days. All perfectly timed, of course so that Mrs. Jemison only suspected the persecution Marie lived with.

She loved school here and she hated it at the same time. She loved it more than she had ever loved school in her life because of Mrs. Jemison, and she hated it more than she ever had before because of Jack Carlson and his gang!

That first day Marie finished helping Mrs. Jemison put out the books, and before the sting of her embarrassment could wear off, the bell rang. In came the children, each staring harder at Marie than the last.

Her face was red with embarrassment as everyone gawked at her. So when Marie caught sight of Sharon her heart gave a leap of relief. Here was a friend at last! Marie beamed a smile of welcome at her new friend. Sharon hesitatingly smiled back, as she slipped into the seat next to her.

Mrs. Jemison began by calling the roll. Marie hardly paid attention as she called out, "Edna." The teacher paused, then called out, "Edna" again.

"Edna—Edna Marie Rhinehart."

Suddenly the room exploded with laughter. Marie looked around to find everyone laughing at her!

With a red face and a timid choked voice she replied, "Here." How she hated that name. Now everyone knew she was named Edna!

She didn't realize Mrs. Jemison would call her that because Mr. Hansen had introduced her as Marie, and Mrs. Jemison had called her Marie when she came to borrow books. The humiliation of it gave shy Marie a courage she could muster, when the need arose.

She raised her hand. Mrs. Jemison ignored it and continued to call roll. Even though everyone in the room continued to laugh Marie kept her hand raised high.

Finally Mrs. Jemison asked, "Yes, Miss Rhinehart?"

"Ah—please, if you please, Mrs. Jemison. My name is Marie."

"Oh, I'm sorry, the roll say's Edna Marie."

"Yes, but if you'd please just call me Marie," her voice lowered to almost an inaudible pitch as she repeated, "please."

As the girls snickered and the boys guffawed, Mrs. Jemison said, "Why certainly, Marie, I'll remember that. Now boys and girls give me your attention."

And for the rest of the morning Mrs. Jemison explained rules and more rules.

Marie tried to get Sharon's attention but she wouldn't even so much as glance at her again. What was wrong? Marie couldn't wait until recess so she could talk to Sharon.

As the morning wore on it became increasingly apparent to Marie that something was terribly wrong between Sharon and herself. The optimism she had felt these last lonely weeks began to fade that first miserable morning at school. First she had to endure the meanness of the boys, then she had to be humiliated by being called Edna, and now this!

She half listened as the teacher's voice droned on and on.

"I hate this place for sure!" she thought as she fought back tears which she simply would NOT allow to come before she could be alone.

Just before the bell, Sharon slipped a note into her hand. "Meet me in the bathroom."

Chapter Six

Sharon went slowly into the bathroom to meet Marie, who had bolted ahead of her. When they both squeezed into the stall, Marie looked hopefully into Sharon's face only to be met with despair.

"Sharon, what's wrong?"

"Oh Marie, you are so funny, I like you so much."

"Well Sharon, is that anything to cry about?"

"I'm sorry Marie, I can't be your friend."

Marie just stood there, nose to nose with Sharon in that bathroom stall, almost not breathing, not daring to ask why, not wanting to know, yet her blue eyes were wild with questions. After what seemed like a long time Sharon spoke, "Marie, my mom won't let me play with you."

"Why?"

"Because—you're not a Mormon, and your dad smokes . . ."

As her voice got lower and trailed off, Marie's mind filled in the rest. "And you live in that filthy farmhouse and you smell like tobacco, your clothes are old, your hair isn't nice and your mom is weird . . ."

"But I am a Mormon. I got baptized same as you when I was eight!"

"Oh Marie! I'm so glad!"

"Well, when she finds out, will she let us be friends?"

Sharon's stricken face said all Marie needed to know. She turned away from Sharon, trying to swallow her humiliation and disappointment.

Sharon started to cry and tried to pull her around, but Marie broke free and ran out the door, down the hall, through the main door and all the way to the barn by Stony Creek Bridge. She went inside, though she was terrified of the place, and found the deepest darkest corner where she tried very hard to curl into a nothing ball.

She held herself tight in this position in the corner—forever, it seemed. She wouldn't allow herself to cry, to think, or feel. She just tried very hard to be nothing.

Finally though, she could feel her arms, legs and neck begin to ache. This brought her to herself and she stretched and looked around at the cool dark shadows in the barn. It didn't seem terrifying like she thought it would, but rather soothing. She pushed her foot into something soft and heard a meow.

"Patches!"

Marie picked up her cat and held him to her cheek. The cat purred and rubbed against Marie's head, which seemed to start her tears.

First they were a slow trickle, but the pressure of her pain was so great it soon broke the dam of hurt and they came flooding out. Earthquakes of sobs followed and racked the young girl for some time. Through it all her cat stayed, watching her with compassion and love, licking her tear-covered hands and meowing from time to time in response to his friend's anguish.

Finally, when the aftershocks subsided to nothing more than shudders followed by a deep sigh, Marie's stomach growled. She began to wonder what time it was and to wonder at what she'd done—Marie had never sluffed school in her life and here she was.

Whatever would she do now, she worried; she couldn't go back to school. She couldn't go home until school was out, either. Just as these thoughts began to form giant fears in her mind, she heard someone calling her name.

That someone was Sharon, the last person on earth Marie wanted to talk to now. She became very silent and waited for her to pass, but Patches seemed to have other ideas. He began meowing his head off.

Marie tried to hush him and whispered, "Be quiet." But she couldn't silence him past Sharon's x-ray hearing and she soon poked her head into the barn.

"Marie, Marie are you in here?"

Marie sat very still, but Patches scrambled out of her lap and ran over to Sharon, where he began rubbing against her leg and meowing loudly.

"You're Marie's cat. Is she here boy?"

Patches seemed determined to announce that she was and immediately bee-lined for Marie in her dark corner. Sharon followed and nearly tripped over Marie.

"Marie, thank goodness I found you—are you OK? Mrs. Jemison and I have been so worried; she sent me out to look for you. After you didn't come back to class, she asked everyone if they had seen you. Course Jack Carlson was delighted to tell her that you were sluffing. I went up to her desk and she took me into her office where I told her what happened. Marie I'm sorry."

Marie wouldn't look up at Sharon. She just stared at her hands in her lap while Sharon continued, "I don't blame you if you never speak to me again. I just want you to know that it's not my fault. I like you lots and I can't make my mom understand what a really nice girl you are.

"She's just sort of, awfully—protective. She doesn't want anything bad to happen to me. Please, Marie, try to understand. Try not to take it so personally."

Marie blurted out, "How would you take it?"

"Yeah."

Sharon sat next to Marie in silence for some time, until Sharon began again, "Marie, I know how you feel about obeying your mother. I like my mom too, but sometimes she's just unreasonable, like now.

"Well, I'd still like to be your friend. We could be secret friends. Marie, it could be so fun. We would be like Romeo and Juliet, bosom friends parted by our parents' silly feud! We can send secret messages to each other. Oh, we just have to find a secret mailbox, in a tree or something.

"I could sneak away sometimes and we could play again here—in the barn and by the bridge. We could dance in the reeds and climb your wonderful trees! Please Marie, speak to me. Tell me you'll be my secret friend, don't send me away broken-hearted with no hope."

Marie had to laugh then, for there was Sharon kneeling at her feet with her hands on her heart pleading her case. "Well, I would speak if I could get a word in edgewise!"

"Oh, then you will, you will be my friend!"

Sharon jumped up and pulled Marie with her. She grabbed her hands and swung her in a crazy dance all-around the dilapidated barn. The girls laughed and hugged each other until they plopped down on the musty hay to plan their wonderful, secret friendship.

After chattering for a very long time Sharon jumped up, "Oh my gosh, we're supposed to be in school, Mrs.

Jemison is so worried. Quick let's wash your face at the creek and go!"

The girls had to stay after school for a week to make up all the work they missed. Mrs. Jemison was so kind behind her sternness; she already had such a big soft spot for little raga-muffin Marie.

Normally not a woman to put up with any misbehavior, she would purposely leave the room, knowing the girls were talking and giggling instead of working. She would leave for a prudent amount of time, finding things to putter with in her office, and then walk in on them.

Clearing her throat rather loudly, she would state in a mock stern tone, "As you girls cannot seem to stay with your task I can see that you will need to stay after school again tomorrow night to finish."

Then she would beam them her big-bird smile and shoo them home. Mrs. Jemison felt only slightly guilty, knowing that she was fostering their friendship when Sharon's mother had strictly forbidden it. She felt absolutely certain that sweet little Marie could not be much of a bad influence on Sharon.

Chapter Seven

One Saturday afternoon a few weeks later, Marie and Sharon met in the dense thicket near the bridge so that no one could see them playing together. As Marie was dragging Sharon through the brush she said, "I keep thinking we'll find a hole in a tree."

Sharon's face was getting scratched as Marie doggedly dragged her through the brush. Her eyes were squinted and she kept her hands near her face to deflect the limbs Marie was carelessly flipping at her as she passed.

So with rising irritation she asked, "Why?"

Not even noticing her friend's discomfort, Marie replied with her own question, "Didn't you read the book, *Spy On The Playground*?"

"No."

"You don't read enough—anyway the bad guys passed messages to the spy by leaving notes in a hole in a tree—it would be perfect."

"You read too much—and we have been searching for a long time. I can't see any holes in these trees," muttered Sharon.

"We have to find a message center, Sharon. All the good ones I have ever read about are holes in trees, or a secret stone cave, maybe."

Marie had given Sharon an idea and she began

searching on the ground as she called to Marie, "Hey, this is it—come here, Marie!"

Marie walked over to Sharon, who was brushing dirt away from a large flat stone.

"This is perfect."

Marie looked confused.

"Here—give me a hand with this."

Marie bent down and took the stick Sharon handed to her. With their heads bent over the hole, they worked together as frantically as two little ground hogs flipping dirt out behind them. Sharon's long black hair intertwined with Marie's short blonde fluff in the autumn wind, as though each were a part of a fabulous ballet being performed with the bright orange and yellow leaves dancing in the wind around their heads.

The girls worked away—oblivious to the majesty of the leaves swirling as they landed on the dusty ground, dancing a bit, until a large gust of wind like cymbals clashing in an orchestra, would swoop them up to begin the vigorous dance again.

When the hole was sufficiently excavated, Sharon said, "OK, Marie, push."

They gave a great heave and over the stone went. Sharon let out a scream to wake the dead. Marie looked quickly around, expecting any minute to see a band of *boys*, or wild animals.

Seeing nothing, she looked again at her friend who had backed up the hill pointing in disgust at the hole left by the stone. Marie's eyes followed her pointing finger; then she burst out laughing. Squiggly, wiggly little potato bugs were scrambling every which way.

Sharon faced her friend accusingly, "I don't think it's funny."

Seeing Sharon's anger and hurt, Marie quickly apologized. Pulling on her arm she steered her a safe distance from the wigglies and sat them both down.

She did have to make an effort not to smile. Sharon was so funny and they were just little bugs. Marie suppressed her smile and turned to her friend.

"Sharon, what were we doing anyway? Why did you want to turn that big rock over?"

"It reminded me of the Angel Moroni—you know, the buried gold plates?" Now it was Sharon's turn to be astonished. Marie sat there with a totally blank stare.

"Haven't you heard of Moroni?" Marie just shook her head and felt uncomfortable. Sharon asked the question as though Moroni was Elvis Presley—or someone just as famous.

"I thought you were a Mormon. Didn't you get baptized?"

"Yes!"

Marie said defensively, as her mind went back to her baptism three years ago. She had been baptized at the usual age of eight. Her real grandmother, her mother's mother, had seen to it. She remembered walking the many blocks to the old Tabernacle in Price. Her aunt and cousins had been there and they all seemed pretty happy. She had worn her cousin's white dress and was lowered into the warm water by a very nice man.

The next day she had gone to the Mormon Church for the only time she could ever remember. How frightened she had been as she walked all the way to the front of that dark chapel. She had sat on a chair, trembling all over as several men put their hands on her head and flattened her hair, which her aunt had so carefully combed and curled.

They said some words, which she had finally decided was a prayer, then they shook her hand all-round and she had walked to the back of the chapel again.

Her grandmother had taken her home, before the meeting had ended. She remembered feeling reluctant to go and was very curious about what went on, but asked no questions, except why her mother had not come. She couldn't remember the answer, but had decided it must not be very important to her mom.

Though she had not understood anything about the experience of baptism, she did remember a feeling that this was a very important and very good thing she had done.

That day she had felt proud to be a Mormon. And even when she had found out the old grandma hadn't liked her because she was a Mormon, she'd still felt proud, even as she'd wondered what was wrong with them.

Then when the boys at school hadn't liked her because she was a Jack Mormon, she had felt mad. What made her a *Jack* Mormon, anyway? What was a Jack Mormon? All the Jacks she knew were boys, and Jack Carlson was a creep. How could someone call her a *Jack* when she was a girl?

There were simply too many questions for one so young to answer and she had no one to ask. Now Sharon didn't seem very pleased with her either, and all because of this Mormon stuff!

Sharon didn't seem to notice her silence because she was thinking her own thoughts. A light seemed to go on in her head as a new knowledge was born in her young mind. She had never before known anyone who didn't know about Moroni. It was like living in America and not knowing who the President was.

A squirrel stopped to watch the girls, who were being strangely silent and still for human children. When he skittered away it startled both girls.

Sharon spoke first, "Do you know about Joseph Smith?"

Marie just shook her head.

"You don't know about him—well what do you know?"

Feeling huffy and a lot like leaving, Marie said, "I thought I knew you were my friend!"

Now Sharon was confused, "Course you are—wha'd'ya' mean?"

"Well, I'm not stupid. How could I know about all these people if no one ever told me?" By now Marie was on her feet with her hands on her hips.

Now it was Sharon's turn to apologize. This time she put her arm around her friend and steered her back to their perch on the creek bank, as she earnestly tried to explain what she understood about the Book of Mormon and Joseph Smith.

As Marie listened to Sharon's tale, told with childlike sincerity, she loved it.

"So Mormons weren't something terrible. I just knew that old fat grandma didn't know anything about Mormons," she thought with great relief.

She immediately began to long for a copy of the Book of Mormon to read for herself. She was positive she had never seen it at the school library. It had never entered her mind to buy one. She didn't own many books. When you needed as many things as Marie's family did, you didn't buy books. She would never, NEVER ask a friend to borrow a book—except from a library, because adults thought you were wonderful when you wanted to borrow books from libraries.

On the other hand they thought you were *very bad* if you wanted to borrow anything else. The only other thing she had ever borrowed was bread—and that was awful. You only borrowed bread when you were terribly hungry. She would never humiliate herself by borrowing a book, even as much as Marie cherished books.

So she tucked that sudden longing away where it belonged, in a nice dark corner of her cedar chest of dreams, and gave her full attention back to Sharon.

"That's really a nice story, Sharon. I'm glad you told me; I liked it a lot, but what does it have to do with this stone?"

"Don't you get it? Our message place could be a box buried under a stone!"

Marie's imagination leaped on the idea. As she hugged Sharon for joy, she exclaimed, "What a great idea, and I have just the box."

Before Sharon could get another word in, Marie was heading for home, breathlessly telling Sharon to wait right there as she ran.

She dashed in the door, bolted for her room, dived under her bed and grabbed a box. She emptied the contents onto the bed and ran through the house before her mother could detain her. Ten minutes later she slid into home base at Sharon's feet, panting breathlessly and grinning from ear to ear. She pushed the box at her friend.

Sharon looked aghast at the colorfully painted "Marlboro Man" on his horse, with a cowboy hat on his head, spurs on his boots, and a big oversized cigar in his mouth. Marie didn't notice her discomfort as she took the box from Sharon and began to explain it's marvels.

"It's great—look! See, it's made out of wood and it has this wonderful top that opens like a book. It fits real snug and tight and . . ." Marie's words trailed off as she looked at Sharon's stern face. All she could blurt out was, "What?"

"We can't use this!"

"Why not?"

"Because it's a cigar box!"

"So . . . ?"

"Marie, don't you know anything? Don't you know Mormons don't smoke?"

Marie was getting testy, "Sharon, I didn't know about Moroni and I didn't know about Joseph Smith, but of course I *know* Mormons don't smoke. I didn't say let's smoke the box, I just said let's bury it. So?"

"So we can't bury a cigar box under a rock that looks like Moroni's rock. It . . ." She wanted desperately for Marie to understand. "It—well—oh just imagine, our messages and special things would smell—like cigars!"

"You mean like me," Marie said quietly.

Sharon immediately felt terrible, "No—not—Marie wait!" She grabbed at her arm as Marie began pushing herself up.

"Wait—you goose! I didn't mean to hurt your feelings. It's just a box!" She took the box and squeaked open the snug lid, her mind searching frantically for a way to retrieve the situation.

"It doesn't matter, we can bury it now. Next time I come I can bring some pretty calico fabric left over from my new dress to cover it with, and I'll squirt mamma's perfume all over the material so it will smell wonderful!"

Marie pushed Sharon's hand from her arm and stood up to leave. Sharon lunged for Marie again, but teetered back stepping right into the hole. She jumped and started flipping her foot and squealing.

She looked so funny Marie could not stop herself from laughing. She laughed harder as she brushed bugs off Sharon's foot. Sharon began laughing as she fell over on the ditch bank. They laughed harder as Sharon's fall pulled Marie onto the cold ground.

The fall seemed to bump them back into the world of time. They suddenly realized how cold the wind was as it bit through their thin jackets.

"Marie, I have to go; I've been gone much longer than I thought."

Sharon had to go, yet the girls both sat on the hard, cold ground in silence for awhile, neither willing to end it this way.

Finally Sharon grabbed her digging stick and hesitantly headed for the hole. Marie admired Sharon's courage for heading back to the buggy hole and in that moment frankly forgave her. She took Sharon's stick from her hand and quickly scooped out all the bugs and dug out a nice size hole just big enough for the cigar box. Sharon didn't even apologize for not helping, nor did Marie expect it.

She placed the box in the hole, and then looked up expectantly at Sharon as if to say, "Am I forgiven?"

Sharon gave her a broad smile and together they heaved the big stone into place. Without speaking they began to push dirt against the stone, and scatter leaves and twigs all-round it. After that Marie took a branch and swept away their footprints, explaining—to Sharon's wonder—that she had read about that in a book about Indians.

When it had been concealed to their satisfaction, they hugged, and came out of the dense thicket by the creek. After checking for danger, in the form of little brothers or BOYS from school, they gave each other one last grin and headed in opposite directions.

As she went home Marie was so glad she hadn't left before. It was a good thing Sharon got bugs on her foot, she smiled to herself. Even if it still hurt to be branded by the smell of cigarettes, she wholeheartedly forgave Sharon as she thought about the wonderful story of Joseph Smith and Moroni.

She felt immense relief that Mormons were really nice and it made her wonder why the old Grandma Giovanni hated them so. Maybe she hated Mormons because they didn't like smoking and her dearest son smoked.

Even though she couldn't answer all questions, she felt like a great many had been answered that day. Perhaps another time Sharon could tell her what a Jack Mormon was.

Marie was young enough to believe with perfect faith that the world was a place of magic. She was innocent enough to accept the visit of an angel without question, but she was *too* young to believe that an angel would really choose to visit a fourteen year old BOY.

"If I were an angel I would have found a nice young girl to visit," she thought happily, as she skipped through the fall leaves toward home.

Chapter Eight

The next day on the way to school Marie was dancing along thinking of best friends, angels and buried boxes when something wet fell on her nose.

She looked up and joyfully stretched out her tongue to catch a snowdrop. As she savored the coolness of it in her mouth, she raised her face again to the sky and watched the flakes begin to swirl. She continued to look up into swirling sky as she walked along, until she had to blink the snowflakes from her eyes.

Just at that moment she bumped her head into the porch rail of a house. She had been so intent on the first snow of the season that she had wandered off the road. Marie teetered for a moment, stunned, then put her hand to her head and began to move back into the street. Again she plowed right into something big and soft.

"Little girl, what have you done?"

Marie looked up into the face of an enormously fat woman and speechlessly began to back away.

The woman put out her hand and moved toward Marie, making her flinch. "What have you done to yourself, little von, you are bleeding, ja?"

Marie looked at her hand which was covered in blood. She realized that her eye felt sticky and her stomach felt funny.

The woman raised her pudgy hand toward Marie again, and as she backed away more quickly, the strange woman shouted, "Stop, stop, little von!"

Marie found herself falling into a great black void as she struggled to understand the meaning of the fat woman's screams, mingled with the screech of tires on pavement and the pain and then blackness.

Marie was brought into the house and laid in a big four poster feather bed. She would have been sad to miss this, for it was the softest bed she had ever been in. The bed was covered in a flowered quilt tied with lavender yarn and smelling fresh and clean. To the right were stiffly starched, white ruffled curtains tied back on sparkling clean windows.

The snow was gently falling and just beginning to stick on the little white framed panes. Marie could remember nothing of this, but instead dreamed she was in the ginger bread house of a wicked witch. A very large witch with flabby arms raised to hit and shouting, "Stop'a that crying—you'a such a bambina . . ."

"Mrs. Giovanni, I'm afraid your daughter has had a bad concussion. She is still unconscious, but her vital signs are good and we can find no broken bones or other internal injuries. We did put a few stitches in her head, but that doesn't look too serious. If she wakes soon she could be all right. We need to keep her, of course, until she is conscious, and all we can do now is watch her and wait."

As the doctor left the shadowy waiting room, he glanced again at the dejected woman slumped in the corner chair. She made him uncomfortable, but he was far too busy to realize that it was because of her tattered maternity dress, unkempt hair and despairing eyes.

Even the nurse found it easier to avoid her than to offer a kind word. She had the fleeting thought that the woman would like to lie down somewhere, but she was tired herself and nearly off duty for the night.

She soothed her conscience by saying to herself, "Well, the next shift will take care of her," and hustled to finish her chores.

The nurse on the next shift came in and at least offered the woman in the waiting room a cheery hello. When she made no response, the nurse self-righteously went about her business, thinking the woman rude, and muttering to herself, "Well, and what did I expect? One only has to look at her and realize that she probably brought her problems on herself. Someone who would wear a dress like that in public just has no pride; and her hair—well!" So this woman too "passed by on the other side," leaving Marie's mother staring at the black and white tiled floor.

"Mrs. Giovanni?" Marie's mother looked up in surprise and hope, but did not see either a nurse or doctor.

"I'm Berta."

When Mrs. Giovanni stared blankly back, she went on, "Berta Bottigheimer, ja. The lady that called the doctor. Your little von, she hurt herself on my porch, poor lamb, and when I wanted to help her she just ran into the street. I think I frightened her; I could not stop her. I am so, so sorry."

"Oh," was all Marie's mother said, and stared again at the tiled floor.

"So how is the little von? She will be OK, ja? Please, what can I do?"

Mrs. Giovanni did not even bother to respond, except a barely perceptible shrug of her shoulder.

“Are you here alone—have you eaten?” But she could get not so much as a shrug this time.

With that Berta Bottigheimer turned quickly on her heel, for such a large woman, and waddled off, muttering to herself. As she huffed and hurried down the hall, the long silky hair of a doll bobbed up and down, as though playing peek-a-boo from a big bag which flip-flopped against her generous side.

Marie’s mother watched her leave for a moment and then sighed and settled down to watch the floor once more. A short time later she nearly jumped out of her skin as a plate of food was shoved under her nose.

“Here, dear, you must eat for the little von on your lap, ja, and for the little von in the hospital bed. Then I must find you a bed also.”

She raised her weary eyes to look into the large kind eyes of a stranger, with a stranger name and a funny accent. She managed a weak smile and stuttered a quiet, awkward thanks. As she raised the hamburger gratefully to her lips and quietly ate, tears formed in her lovely brown eyes.

Berta left with tears in her own and then shortly returned with an orderly, who escorted her to a cot in a corner room. Marie’s mother closed her tired eyes and shivered as a warmed blanket was tenderly tucked around her by very flabby, capable, compassionate arms.

Chapter Nine

Marie opened her eyes to the tender touch of her mother's hand, stroking her hair back off her face. Bright sun was streaming into a strange window and for a moment she imagined herself a tiny girl again, waking from her nap, until her conscious mind registered her terrible headache. Her head hurt more with each stroke of her mother's gentle hand, but she could not tell her to stop for a very long time.

It had been so long since her mother had given her that much attention and tenderness that it was worth the pain it caused. Her tenderness and look of concern were so wonderful that Marie could not stop her tears. After what seemed like a very long time Marie reached for her mother's hand and slowly pulled it away from her throbbing head.

She looked around to find herself in a very strange room. It was painted a horrible shade of green and smelled like a doctor's office. She was in a very high bed with a rail that made it seem like a crib. It gave her that cherished, protected, baby feeling again.

She looked all-round, then back to her mother with a thousand questions, but as always her mother's deep silent nature volunteered nothing.

"Mamma, where am I?"

Before Emma could speak a tall, very bald man, dressed in white, strode into the room.

"So—you're awake are you? I'm Doctor Lane—let's have a look at you."

Marie was pronounced quite healthy—just shaken. She was kept overnight just to be safe and sent home the next day.

At home Marie was bored—thoroughly bored. She was glad not to be in school all the same. She was glad the doctor recommended she miss a whole week because of her accident. It's not every day one is hit by a car. That was exciting to Marie, but she was sorry she couldn't even remember being hit by the car.

All she could remember was running into the fat lady's porch. Who was that fat lady? Fat ladies scared her. She hadn't asked her mother any details and her mother was a woman of very few words. She hadn't told Marie a thing about what happened. She was so depressed and resigned to trouble that she simply brought her child home and put her to bed. She did tell Marie that she was sorry for her, and then she ignored her, relapsing into her morbid depression.

Children bounce back from illness so quickly and Marie was no exception. Even the stitches on her head were soon forgotten. She felt quite well, so she just took care of herself. She didn't even have to do chores, because she had been run over.

The babies had gotten used to playing alone since their big sister was in school, so for the most part, even they left her alone. Marie's mother hadn't been having her do many chores before the accident lately anyway. She just lay around and cried while the housework piled up. Marie would do some dishes without being asked, to try and cheer her up.

She would say, "See mamma, I did the dishes; aren't you glad."

Marie's mother would mutter something and hardly notice. Marie worried so much about her mother. She constantly wondered if she was sad because she wasn't helping enough, or being good enough. Marie had plenty of time to worry that week out of school. She had plenty of time to think, too.

She didn't even have one book in the house she hadn't read. She wished again that she had a copy of the strange golden book Sharon had told her about. For some reason she could not explain, she simply wanted to know more about it and the angel and Joseph Smith. She couldn't go to the library because it was at the school, and she was supposed to be injured!

She was nearly out of her mind when a package arrived from the mailman for her. Just for Marie! A package for her was a very rare event. Sometimes the Grandma Giovanni sent packages for her darling little Tony and Bradley, but nothing was ever included for Marie.

She eagerly tore off the brown paper and was delirious with joy as she picked up a book—until she read the cover, *Grimm's Fairy Tales*. Fairy tales? She hated fairy tales!

Marie had a wonderful imagination. She imagined that her bedroom could be a wonderful new place and she imagined that she could look like a princess. She could even imagine that maybe an angel would really visit a boy, but she could never imagine that a frog could turn into a prince—yuk; that was impossible!

In disappointment she tossed the book onto her bed and noticed a note fall out:

Dear Marie,

I am so sorry about your accident. I did not mean to frighten you, I hope you will enjoy this book while you recover. When I was a child I loved fairy tales, do you believe in fairy tales? Someone very dear to me once told me, that whenever life gets hard, I should just remember to believe in fairy tales.

Perhaps when you feel better you could visit and we could become acquainted. I heard you like to read, do you also like dolls?

Sincerely, Berta Bottigheimer

"Mamma, who is this from?"

Her mother took the note and a brief look of happy surprise filled her face. Marie thought her mother was so beautiful when she looked like that. She always used to look happy, until she married that man and had babies.

"She's the lady who called the doctor. The one whose porch you ran into."

"Her! Why is she sending me something?"

"Why, Marie, she was very kind to do so. She was very kind to me while you were in the hospital too." Without further explanation she handed Marie the note and left the room.

Why had she sent Marie a gift; what did she want anyway? Was she for real? That big fat old lady believed in fairy tales, and what did she mean, do I like dolls? Marie felt even more afraid of this woman. She definitely would not read her book and she definitely would not go to see her.

Somewhere in the back of her little girl's mind, Marie

was afraid that witches just might exist. From what she knew of them, they always lied to children to get them into their Gingerbread Houses. No! She would not go into that woman's pretty little house ever again.

Marie's boredom was more than she could stand on her third day home. Anytime Marie's mind had leisure to wander, like her bored days at home, her mind went back to Sharon's strange story about the Angel Moroni and the buried box. About three-thirty that afternoon she was in her room thinking about it, when little Tony came into her bedroom carrying a muddy piece of paper.

"Tony what is that thing? Get it out of my room right now."

"No," said Tony stubbornly.

"Tony," said Marie with a threat in her voice.

"No. A girl give it to me. She give me a piece a candy too if I promised to give it to you and then I fell down in the mud. Here!" He shoved his chubby little hand with the grubby paper clutched in it at Marie. She took it from him and carefully unwrapped it.

Dear Marie,

You must get back to school as fast as you can. I hope you are better because I know you can't wait to hear what we are doing. You will just die for joy! Oh and how are your . . . She couldn't make out the middle of the note because it was smudged with mud, but the rest of it continued . . . *I sure hope so, you'll need them!*

Love your best secret friend, Sharon

As a puzzled Marie folded the muddy wet note up, she noticed more writing on the back side.

P.S. I was going to . . . more mud *. . . secret cigar box. But I couldn't stand to dig up the squiggly bugs all alone. Did you leave me a note in it?*

"Why," thought Marie, "I forgot all about our buried box! What if Sharon had left the note there? How lucky," she chuckled to herself, "that Sharon was so timid about a few bugs!"

That did it—Marie'd had enough of being sick. She felt fine since coming home and now she had to convince her mother she was ready to go back to school!

Chapter Ten

Sharon never could bring herself to dig that box back up, and Marie—if the truth be told—was still touchy about Sharon's reaction to the cigar box. After that they simply passed each other notes at school.

When Marie went back to school after her accident she learned Mrs. Jemison had made an announcement that took Marie's breath away; they would be having their annual Christmas Pageant at the church and everyone in town would be invited!

In her old school, Christmas Programs were only practiced a few weeks before the event, but here they started months ahead. Each grade had an assignment and Marie could not believe her ears when she heard what the sixth grade would do. The three girls would be dancing—dancing!

All her life Marie had wanted to dance on a real stage, to prance and twirl in front of a real audience. As the morning's work began, Marie could not take her mind off the wonder of the Christmas Pageant.

The classroom disappeared and she saw the whole thing in vision. *She was the star, dancing in the middle with Joan and Sharon on either side, accenting her every wonderful move. The music ended, the crowd clapped and clapped and clapped as they bowed and ran off stage!*

"Marie—Marie Rhinehart."

Marie jumped in her chair and looked surprised to find herself in class.

"Marie, please read paragraph four."

"Boy, how had they gotten this far into their reading assignment?" Marie must have been daydreaming for at least fifteen minutes. She took out her book and had to ask what page they were on.

The girls giggled and the boys jeered. Marie turned a bright red as Mrs. Jemison called the class to order, while Marie found her place, then she squared her shoulders and in her most dramatic voice read the words with all the feeling and dignity she could muster.

That recess in the bathroom Sharon and Marie did a jig around the bathroom stall, up over the toilet and down to the floor, again and again. They couldn't contain their joy, until someone else came in. They each grabbed the other's mouth for silence. Marie scrambled to stand on the toilet seat and bend over so it looked like only one person was in the stall. Joan Dobbs walked in and called out.

"Sharon, is that you?"

The girls in the stall looked at each other with red puffy faces barely able to contain their glee. Carefully Marie removed her hand from Sharon's mouth.

"Yes, what do you want?" Sharon asked, trying to sound as normal as possible.

"Come out here and talk to me."

Sharon thought fast, "I can't. I'm busy."

Joan couldn't wait so she talked to Sharon through the door. "Did you hear what Mrs. Jemison said? Can you believe it? I'm not going to dance with that Jack Mormon anywhere, but especially *not* at the church. Thank goodness your mother will never allow you to!"

Both girls were shocked as Sharon looked apologetically at Marie. Marie felt like she'd been slapped in the face and her eyes fell before Sharon's.

Sharon felt angry as she replied, "That is the meanest thing I've ever heard Joan. Marie has as much right to dance as you do."

"Then maybe she should do a solo."

"Maybe she should; I'm going to tell Mrs. Jemison."

"Well, maybe I could tell your mother how eager you are to spend time with that white trash girl!"

"You do that and I'm certain when Mrs. Jemison hears how you feel she'll give you another part. Maybe you could carry on props for Marie and me when we dance."

"She *is* the teacher's pet. Well, if she can dance, so can I. Just don't be surprised if she trips once or twice on stage," Joan said as she slammed the bathroom door shut.

As the girls came silently out of the stall, Sharon said, "Marie, I'm sorry."

"It's OK. You go in now and I'll come in a minute. And thanks, Sharon—thanks for sticking up for me."

Sharon didn't know what else to say so she turned to leave. As an afterthought Marie grabbed her arm and asked, "Sharon, just what is a Jack Mormon anyway?"

"I'm not sure, it's probably not a very good person, ah you know."

"Like someone who smokes?"

"Yeah, I guess."

"But I don't."

"I know, Joan's just stupid and so is Jack Carlson."

Marie gave Sharon a little hug and said, "Thanks, Sharon." Sharon left and she went back into the stall and wiped her eyes, mumbling about those tears.

She swallowed down the hurt quickly and refused to feel bad. She kept reminding herself that she would dance. She would dance and dance on a real stage, with her true "Bosom Friend" for her admiring audience of Mrs. Jemison and Mr. Hansen and her Mamma.

Whenever people were unkind to her, Marie would feel so bad. She hated contention, especially when someone hypocritically tried to "pretend" that *all was well.* When someone was forthright in their feelings about you, well it hurt, but at least it was honest. She hated the undercurrents created by hypocrisy like Joan's, and Marie was always discerning enough to detect it.

Usually she would be meek and nice to the person, to try and mend the situation. During the next few weeks as the girls stayed after school to practice their dance, she tried very hard to appease Joan. Joan, of course, did not know that Marie knew of her true feelings. She was cold but courteous to Marie and wondered why she was so nice. Didn't she get tired of being nice?

Joan decided to ignore her and try to get Sharon's attention. She had always wanted Sharon's attention, but since first grade the two hadn't hit it off and she felt jealous that Sharon seemed to share some secret joy with an outsider like Marie Rhinehart.

Mrs. Jemison noticed the tension and felt sorry for each little girl as they tried so hard to find their place with each other. She made practices as fun and energetic in her witty, bird-like way as possible. In spite of the undercurrents, Marie enjoyed them more and more. She glowed under Mrs. Jemison's praise, as she asked if Marie had been given dance lessons before, and she glowed even more at her astonishment that she had not.

Marie had never looked forward to anything so much in her life. She almost couldn't sleep at night for the joy of dancing in the coming Christmas Pageant!

Chapter Eleven

If things were getting better at school, life at home just seemed to get worse. No one ever talked to her at home and this weekend had been especially bad.

Her parents yelled at her and at each other, but there were never explanations for all the discord, only evidence of their troubles—like the corn meal mush they were having for dinner again tonight. The mush was awful, without salt, with a definite tobacco smoke flavor, and lumpy. However, the taste of the mush wasn't as bad as the way it was served. The family never had meals at the table. Marie felt so sorry for her tired mother.

She stood at the stove, slumped really, stirring the mush. She stopped often to stare with her sad eyes at nothing—then she sighed, then stirred a little more, then she pressed her hand hard into her back, and stared at nothing again. She opened a can of tomato paste and poured it over the mess. Then she hoisted the big heavy pot onto her hip and waddled with it into the living room where Antonio, Marie's stepfather, was lying on the worn and tattered couch, smoking and watching T.V.

An old chair with its back missing, its vinyl torn, and dirty cotton stuffing hanging out, was kept by the side of the couch. Her mother plopped the pot down on the chair and handed him a spoon.

Then, as they always did, the family lined up with bowls in hand for soup. Marie hated this. She felt like a beggar must feel in a charity soup line. While waiting in line Antonio made crude, unjust, and unkind remarks about his fat wife's lack of grooming and cooking.

Marie tried hard to stare straight ahead, directing her contempt instead at the gruesome deer head hanging on the wall behind the couch. Its big brown glass eyes stared back, making her feel that it would be ready to gore anyone who dared to defy its master. But when the hot mush splattered on her hand, as it often did, Marie's disgust was too much for her temper. She quickly spit back a retort in her mother's defense, which was just what Antonio wanted as he chuckled and grinned his delight at the "little spitfire." This scene was played out all too often anymore.

Marie learned what she could about their troubles from eavesdropping. She didn't understand most of what they talked about, except that her stepfather had lost his job at the coal mine again. Marie's hospital bill didn't help matters much. Her guilt and sorrow over bringing more trouble to her mother were almost more than she could bear.

She promised herself that she would try to quit daydreaming so much and pay attention. If she had paid attention, she would never have run into that scary woman's porch! Because of it, it would be a long time—who knew when?—when they would have enough money again. Maybe even the mush would run out, and they would be put out of the farmhouse.

To escape, Marie imagined herself and her mother living happily together in a nice abandoned "boxcar" as the *Boxcar Children* had.

But the day they had all dreaded came. The corn meal

was gone. The tomato paste was long gone. Even the coffee was almost gone.

"At least," thought Marie, "we still have enough wood to burn for warmth."

No matter—they would eat soon, because her stepfather was coming home tonight with food. Marie tried to distract the hungry little boys with stories as they waited. Before long they could hear his pick-up coming down the lane. Marie's mother came out of the bedroom, smoothed back her hair and cotton house dress.

The little boys ran eagerly to the door shouting, "Daddy, Daddy!"

Marie stood at a safe distance, eagerly awaiting his entrance, but their looks of anticipation soon disappeared. Antonio came in looking dejected.

Marie bee-lined for her room. She didn't want to be there for the inevitable fight; she huddled in the dim corner of her bedroom and listened. She waited for the ruckus, but all she could hear were lowered voices. Soon her mother tapped on her door. Marie knew what was coming.

"Why me? How come I have to be the one? I always have to go. He should go. He was the one who didn't bring home any food," thought Marie resentfully as her mother explained her errand.

She didn't express any of this vocally; she just put on her coat and set out. She had already been to the Adams to borrow bread many times—too many times lately.

Once she asked her mother to let her go to Mr. Hansen instead, but she was hushed instantly. If they had *some* money she could shop in Mr. Hansen's store, but they wouldn't go to him without a cent.

She couldn't figure out the difference. In fact, he was

ever so much kinder to her than the Adams. They were getting so old and feeble, they could hardly walk to the door. She could feel that they really didn't appreciate her asking, and it made it so hard to do, but she said none of this to her mother as she left.

Marie's mother told her to hurry before the storm got worse. Then almost as an afterthought Emma said, "Why don't you go to that nice lady who called the doctor for us? What was her name—Mrs. Botig-i . . . whatever her name was—I think she'd help."

Marie hurried off as though she hadn't heard. As she left the house and began down the lane a beautiful, fluffy white snow was gently falling. Everything was very hushed and beautiful as the snow fell on an already white world.

She had no intention of going to Mrs. Botti-something's house. Marie was even more certain than ever that she was a witch.

She'd had a long talk with Sharon about that woman, and the things she'd learned! Why, she wasn't even a Mormon—just like old lady Giovanni! She drank coffee, but all the kids were certain it was actually witch's brew. Marie's family drank coffee, but that was different—it was just coffee!

The kids in town weren't allowed to go near her place because she might teach them incorrect doctrine (whatever that was), and she made dolls. Sharon's mother said any woman of her age, in her right mind, would stop playing with dolls. It was proof positive that she was "touched" in the head!

Marie decided to take a short cut through the fields to save time. As she turned off the lane and walked on, her mind was deep in thought. She thought about the things Sharon had said about Mrs. Bott-i-ig whatever the name was. Marie could never pronounce her name and decided to call her Mrs. Botti. Marie also thought about the Angel Moroni and Joseph Smith.

Marie's thoughts were interrupted as the wind slapped her wet scarf into her face. The rough edges hit her eye making it sting and water. She hadn't even noticed the wind—it was getting mean. Even the snow wasn't gentle now as it swirled around her. As she looked up into the blackness, the snow seemed to move up and away from her almost into a tunnel high above her head, then it would change course and swoop down into her face.

Marie stopped to look around and get her bearings. She looked but could not recognize anything familiar—not the big wind break trees, or the ditch, or even the haystack. Everything was the same black and white forever!

She wanted to go home. She wanted her mother! She started to run, tripped on a clod and fell. Her heart was beating very fast; she knew she was lost.

Her mind kept saying, "What shall I do? Who will help me?"

Suddenly she remembered about Joseph Smith. Sharon had said, when he didn't know what to do, he prayed to God. Marie had never done that before in her life, but without moving from the spot and without hesitation, she now asked for help. It was a simple child's prayer, filled with faith.

"Dear God, if you're real like Sharon said, if you helped a *boy* like Sharon said, please help me—even though I'm just a girl; I need to find my way home."

As she raised her eyes she saw a light flick on in the

distance. Her heart began pounding with an absolute knowledge that the light had been turned on just for her!

Mr. Adams had just finished eating dinner and settled in his comfortable chair. His wife brought him the evening paper and a good cup of hot cocoa. He read a few sentences, but he couldn't continue—he had a most distinct impression to go check on his cows. He pushed the thought aside since he hadn't finished the milking more than forty minutes ago.

He read a bit and then finally tossed the paper down. He pulled on his heavy boots and coat and headed for the barn where he flicked on a light and looked around. Everything seemed fine.

He turned around to go back, muttering in disgust, "I'm an ole' fool. Maybe I ought to sell this place, 'n get me a rockin' chair." Then he heard a noise and nearly dropped his lantern as a wet little urchin stumbled into the barn.

"Mr. Adams?"

"What in the . . .? It's a girl. What in the world are you doing out on a night like this?" His words, spoken with a stinging reprimand, scared Marie into silence.

"Well?" Mr. Adams always shouted because he was losing his hearing.

Marie gathered her courage and mumbled her errand.

"What—what's that you're saying, girl?"

Marie asked him for bread again—louder this time.

Mr. Adams grumbled his displeasure, saying he didn't think they had any bread in the house anyway. Marie fought back her tears and the desire to run and followed him to the house.

She waited on the back step, fighting the wind and snow for what seemed an eternity; finally he came back to the door. He shoved a loaf at her, saying Mrs. Adams had found one in the freezer that he supposed they could spare, then shut and locked the door.

Marie clutched the frozen loaf with a mumbled "Thanks," and ran out of his yard, straight into the storm. Mr. Adams closed the door. Grumbling and muttering to himself, he nearly tripped over his wife as he returned to his comfortable chair.

"What ruffled your feathers?"

As he settled back and reached for his cup, he wrinkled his nose with displeasure at the now cold cocoa. "Oh nothin', I was just thinkin' about that girl. Those kind are all alike. Seems to me that so-called father of hers ought to get himself a job instead of botherin' poor old folks like us. What does he think—I can feed us an' them too? Why, we just have our social see-curity now to live on.

"Course, this place is comfortable and warm. Bessy—she gives right rich milk. Makes a man proud, mother, it does. I worked hard all my life for what I got. Seems like that father of hern' ought to work too. If'n he did, he'd not have to come a beggin'. He'd have a nice spread like mine. Yes sir, it ain't right somehow, it ain't right."

"Well, Mr. Adams, it don't seem right to send a little girl, somehow. It seems to me he ought to have come hisself, if he has the *nerve* to ask for bread."

"Mother, it's like I always said, 'the apple don't fall far from the tree.' Take my word for it."

"Could be you're right," Mrs. Adams mumbled as she knocked a dusty book off the end table. She picked it up and wiped it with her sleeve.

Oh my, she thought, "I'm gettin' old to let things get this dusty."

She put it back in the place it had sat for so long and reached out to turn on the T.V. for the evening news. The stories of murder and the fight on Capitol Hill over new taxes, drowned out the words whispering from the dusty book.

"And also, ye yourselves will succor those that stand in need of your succor; ye will administer of your substance unto him that standeth in need; and ye will not suffer that the beggar putteth up his petition to you in vain, and turn him out to perish.

"Perhaps thou shalt say: The man has brought upon himself his misery; therefore I will stay my hand, and will not give unto him of my food, nor impart unto him of my substance that he may not suffer, for his punishments are just—

"But I say unto you, O man, whosoever doeth this the same hath great cause to repent . . . For behold are we not all beggars?"

Later that night as they retired to bed, they prayed with gratitude that they were not as their lazy neighbors, and thanked the Lord for all the bounties for which they had worked so hard to make their life, in their old age, pleasant.

While they prayed, the dusty book whispered, *"For they had a place built up in the center of their synagogue, a place for standing, which was high above the head . . .*

"Therefore, whosoever desired to worship must go forth and stand upon the top thereof, and stretch forth his hands towards heaven, and cry with a loud voice, saying: Holy God, we believe that thou hast separated us from our brethren . . .

"We believe that thou hast elected us to be thy holy children . . ."

But their prayer of pride drowned out the whispers of the dusty book—the book, so longed for by the young girl who would fall asleep that night with the comfort of their small piece of frozen bread; the young girl who earlier that evening had run blindly into the storm after leaving their home; the girl who, upon finding herself lost again, had stopped dead in her tracks.

Before Marie's mind had even formed the question, a voice inside her said, *"Follow the fence posts home."*

Marie could only see one fence post but hurried toward it and just as she reached it she could see another. As she followed the posts home, one at a time, her heart swelled with the same warm feeling, the same sure knowledge she'd had about the light in the dark. As surely as it had been turned on just for her, the same power was guiding her safely home!

At home Marie's mother did not even try to thaw the bread but sliced it frozen and passed everyone *one* large piece. Marie wondered if the bread was magic, because nothing had ever tasted as good as that frozen bread!

Nor had Marie ever felt anything so warm as the glow from the light sent from heaven in response to her first uttered prayer!

Chapter Twelve

That night, with only frozen bread for supper, was the worst. After that her stepfather picked up some temporary work, so they managed to get more corn meal and a few other supplies. Marie was sent periodically to Mr. Hansen's store and somehow they got along.

To be without enough dinner had become so common that Marie didn't spend too much time worrying about it, except on the nights she felt especially hungry. She had much more important things to think about, like the Christmas Pageant!

In fact, she had been so caught up in the wonder of the Christmas Pageant that she had almost forgotten about the baby until the day she came hustling into the house after school, eager to remove her coat and boots. She carelessly stomped snow into the living room and was shocked into silence as she heard a familiar voice.

"You girl, that'sa no way to treat your mamma's floor. Get that snow off'a the floor."

Marie was stunned to see the old grandmamma obliterating the door into the kitchen, flapping her big arms and gesturing Marie back outside. She backed out and slammed the door shut behind her. She sat on the step and sighed. As usual, nothing had been said to her about that woman coming—nothing.

Marie's anger was rising as she thought of all the times in her life her mother had never told her anything. She never explained anything—and now this! Resentment about her mother's marriage, about their sudden move so far away from her other grandma, about her toys, just boiled up in Marie. The anger got bigger and bigger as she jumped off the step and stomped to the outhouse.

She hated that place. She used it quickly and afterward, just could not bring herself to go back into that tiny house. How tiny it would be now, with that monstrous woman in it. Where in the world would she sleep? She knew the only place she could sleep was in Marie's bed. Yuk! The real question was where would Marie sleep? She already knew the answer to her question—on the couch.

Marie stomped to the dilapidated sheds behind the house. She huddled into the driest corner she could find and hunkered down to think and cry and remember. Maybe because Christmas was coming her mind went to her toys. She had blocked them out of her mind so completely because it hurt too much. She hadn't even put their memory into her cedar chest. She never wanted to see it again, but here it was. That awful grandma and Christmas had dragged it out of her and so she succumbed to its pain, as her mind's eye took her into the musty, dark, spidery cellar again.

She saw the canvas cover that held her precious toys prisoner. She wept freezing tears as her mind lifted the cover to reveal all the dear things. There was her little pink stove that got warm when you plugged it in, whose oven was filled with her little pots and pans.

Flopped on top were her dolls—her baby doll with the yellow pajamas and soft cuddly body, her big lady doll and box of paper dolls, and her dear ballerina—her favorite doll. Where was her toy ironing board and iron? She sobbed openly now as she remembered again that it was gone!

The awful memory of that moving day! When her mother had brought her home to find their things being carried out of the house, she ran to her room to search for her toys. The closet was bare! Frantically she ran to find her mother and ask if they were on the truck. No, we don't have room. Why? Why had they been stored in Giovanni's cellar?

Marie hadn't waited for more explanation. She ran the three blocks to the old grandma's house. She pulled and rattled and shook the tall sturdy gate to the back yard, but it did not yield to her frantic efforts. Undaunted she shinnied up the fence and dropped down on the other side, grateful they didn't have a dog!

With superhuman strength, no eleven-year-old should have, she heaved the heavy cellar door open and dived, pell-mell, into the musty scary place.

She knocked things over and cried as she stumbled and searched for her precious belongings. Finally she found them, under the canvas tarp, all but the ironing board and iron. Her mother found her there, sobbing and rocking her soft baby doll in her little rocking chair.

"Where is my ironing board, mamma?"

Her mother assured her that it was somewhere, and they would only store her things here for awhile. Emma pulled the doll from Marie's arms and carried her up the dusty stairs, then walked the sad little girl home.

That last morning, just before they pulled away, Marie heard the old grandmamma arguing with her mother. She had given the ironing board and iron to Anginette! "Marie—she's such a bambina. She's much'a too big a girl for dolls and toys. I told'a my Sally to come last night and take'a the rest. Her little bambina's can use'a the toys."

"You had no right to do that!" Marie's mother shouted.

The old grandmamma had just kissed her precious Antonio and waddled away as they drove off.

"Meow."

"Oh Patches, you dear old Patches." Marie shoved her cold, cold nose into Patches' warm furry tummy, until all her tears were gone. Then she made the warm soft place in her heart turn back into stone and closed the cellar door in her mind.

"Well Patches, I'm glad to see you!" She stroked the cat again and again warming her hands. Finally, reluctantly, she headed for the house.

Her mother was not home. She'd had the baby about ten that morning. Marie could not believe she had been in labor that morning and had said nothing to her. The grandma had driven the three hours to their town and arrived in time to make *her Antonio* a decent meal, with food she had purchased at Hansen's store.

The dirty house and lack of food was wonderful material for a tirade of indignation on behalf of her dear boy. "Ach, Antonio, if you had only married a nice'a Italian girl, in'a the church. It is the Mother Mary's punishment . . ." She would lament as she flapped her arms at him.

"Oh, Mamma," was all he'd say.

Marie just shut it out, did as she was told, and tried to feel nothing. Before she shoved the anger deep, deep, inside and enveloped herself with a numbness, she allowed herself to wonder about the Christmas Pageant. She wouldn't dance if the old fat grandma came; she just wouldn't, and that was that!

As she lay sleepless on the couch that long night, the wonder of what had happened hit. Her mother had a baby girl! Marie had just assumed it would be another boy. Another baby boy to feed and change and tend. Baby boys were adorable, it was true, but you couldn't escape the fact they would grow into mean, big boys.

A baby girl! Marie found herself wondering what she looked like. Would she, could she, look like her? Her little brothers had dark curly hair and olive skin like their father. Would it be possible to have a blonde little sister? All night long she wondered.

In the morning Marie did something she had never done before in her life. She slipped into her mother's room while Antonio was having a breakfast of bacon, eggs, potatoes, toast and juice, with his mamma. She opened Emma's top drawer and lifted the lid on her cigar box; inside was some change. As she quickly gathered some and stuffed it into her shoe, she felt like a thief!

She would tell her mother later that she had borrowed it. She knew her mother couldn't afford something as extravagant as she had planned, but she couldn't help it. The joy and wonder of having a sister were just too much, so off she went to school with the money pinching her foot all day!

Marie completely forgot herself. She completely forgot that she was not back in her old town, with neighbors who played with her and liked her. So overcome was she by the news that she had a sister, that she did the unthinkable. She announced to the whole class, boys and all, that she, Marie

Rhinehart, was having a party at her house after school! A birthday party for her new little sister! The other children were as astonished as Marie was, with her announcement.

Their curiosity about that old farmhouse and the non-member stepfather who smoked was certainly kindled. No one said they would come and no one said they wouldn't. In her incredible mood, Marie took it as acceptance.

After school she hustled into Mr. Hansen's store, "Mr. Hansen, Mr. Hansen!"

"Whoa—is that Marie? I haven't seen you in here for awhile. How are you?" He beamed Marie his biggest smile of welcome.

"Oh I'm just fine! Mr. Hansen my mother had a baby yesterday! A girl!"

"Well, now that's wonderful Marie—real nice." He paused to smile some more. "What can I do for you then?"

"Oh I must hurry, I'm having a party—to celebrate you know! I need to buy a treat for it."

As she spoke her eyes were busy scanning the small food isles until they jumped on a box of vanilla wafers.

"That's it!" She quickly checked the price and saw that she had enough money, which she plunked down with the box of cookies, then wiggled with impatience as Mr. Hansen rang it up.

By the time he turned to reach for the candy jar, she was already streaking through the door, shouting a happy goodbye without even a look back. Her happiness warmed Mr. Hansen through to his toes, and he beamed another smile at her vanishing form, wishing her Godspeed!

Out in front of her house Marie sat waiting hopefully with her box of vanilla wafers clutched to her breast, wondering at herself. What had ever possessed her to have a party? A party at her house no less! A party at her house with the big grandmamma present! She didn't wait long before she saw them coming—the whole class, fourth, fifth and sixth grades coming down her lane!

As the children came, they marveled too. What had possessed them to come? What had possessed them to come to a party at Marie Rhinehart's house, no less? They didn't understand that they were being carried along by her exuberance, and their curiosity.

As they approached Marie, she joyfully opened her box of cookies, generously passing them out. The children, boys and girls alike said nothing, not a word was exchanged by anyone. They just grabbed some cookies, stuffed their mouths as they looked with wide eyes around the haunted place. They quickly ate the cookies, took a last look around and headed back down the road!

Never had there been a stranger ten minute party.

Chapter Thirteen

As little Rose lay sleeping in Marie's arms, she felt heavy and wonderful. Marie loved her instantly, even with her coal black hair and dark little eyes! She wiggled and made a sucking motion with her rosebud mouth, then settled quietly again. Marie was thrilled with the wonder of her small dark eyelashes against her velvet face and her little button of a nose. She had perfect tiny slender hands with teeny tiny fingernails, and perfect little toes!

Marie had held babies before—after all her mother already had two little boys—but she had never held a baby girl before. Someone else might argue that at that tender age there isn't much difference, but Marie knew there certainly was.

For one thing this little mite had much smaller hands and feet. Her hands were slender and feminine in a way that her chubby little brothers never were. Even her name, Rosalee, was feminine, and Marie knew that she would grow up sweet and kind and sensitive, not mischievous and mean like boys did.

As her thoughts about the baby began to ramble in her head, she heard little Tony and Bradley squealing and playing in the other room. A big wave of guilt washed over her and she felt intense disloyalty to her little brothers. She remembered the first time she held each of them and the love she felt then was almost as wondrous—almost.

It was the "almost" that made her resolve to put the baby back in her bed and give each of those cute boys a big squeeze before she gathered her things and left for school!

She felt quite happy as she left that morning. She had a sister, her mother was home and her step grandmother was gone! She didn't even feel a twinge of guilt for being glad about that, even if she wouldn't be there to buy groceries anymore.

She was glad, too, that life at school was getting easier. Marie's newness was wearing off and the boys teased and tormented her less often, but more than anything, Sharon's friendship made her intensely happy. Not just when she and Sharon met secretly to play, but for days and days afterward, the memories of it sustained her.

It was a wonderful thing to know someone loved you. Marie felt secure knowing now that Sharon did. She knew too, that, Mrs. Jemison did, and she felt that Mr. Hansen loved her too. Even the hardest life was made bearable when one had friends. Amazing, she thought, she had friends you could touch and talk to now, not just friends between the pages of books. Not that Marie would neglect old friends for new; she still spent many lovely hours buried in books.

It was a good thing she had her books, because even with the joy of the new baby, things were still plenty tense at home, especially when there wasn't enough to eat. Marie was becoming very expert at blocking all this from her mind when it had more joyful things to think about.

One thing she would never, ever, do was talk about her home life to anyone. Marie was not so young she could not feel shame, and when you felt shamed, you buried it—

deep. That's what made that day before Halloween so very awful.

It was lunchtime and Marie was at her desk without lunch again. In the two-room school it was impossible to get lost in the crowd. When you didn't have a lunch, everyone knew it. Sometimes Sharon would slip her an apple and scold her for forgetting again. Mrs. Jemison had given her parts of her lunch for weeks, until that awful day she asked Marie to come to her desk.

"Marie, did you forget your lunch again?"

"Yes, Mrs. Jemison." Marie spoke with her nose almost dragging on Mrs. Jemison books lined up on the edge of her desk.

Kindly Mrs. Jemison pried, "Marie, how could you forget again?"

Lowering her voice to a bare whisper she asked, "Doesn't your mother have anything to send with you?"

Marie's whole body slumped even deeper. Without looking up she didn't say a thing.

"Marie, please answer me."

Marie couldn't answer. She could never lie to anyone, ever, and never to Mrs. Jemison. Instead, her dread enemy the tears just silently rolled off her chin. It's funny how even in awful moments your mind can think of other things. Marie thought in amazement of how her body could produce such buckets of tears instantly. Oh, to be able to disappear!

Mrs. Jemison handed her a kleenex and excused her from the room; out she went with twenty eyes staring at her. Now she truly understood *Anne of Green Gables*—like Anne, she was—in the depths of despair."

She dried her tears, squared her shoulders and went

back in after lunch recess. She ignored the whispers and got on with life. After school Mrs. Jemison apologized for talking with her in front of the class, as she hugged her and told her of her love and concern. Marie knew that already, and was just sorry for her shame.

Later that night Mrs. Jemison came to Marie's home. Marie was told to gather clothes off the line and missed the whole thing, but she knew it was about her lack of lunch. Oh, she felt sad and sorry that she had to bring more trouble on her poor mother. After Mrs. Jemison left Marie tried to explain.

"Mamma, I'm sorry. I didn't tell her, she just noticed. I'm sorry . . ."

"I know, Marie—well I suppose some good came from it. She said that you will be getting hot lunch from now on."

"Mamma, you can't afford it!"

"Well don't you worry none; just eat the lunch."

Marie's mother gave her a faint teary smile and smoothed her hair gently back from her worried face, the way she used to do every night as she tucked her into bed. As she left the room Marie knew she would get no more information.

Of course through eavesdropping, Marie found out that the Bishop was buying her lunch. She had no idea what a Bishop was; she knew he wasn't part of a chess game she had read about, because this one had many children and was just a poor farmer. Whatever he was, she got the feeling from listening to her mother that he was kind. A special kind of farmer—probably like Mr. Hansen. She even wondered if Mr. Hansen was the Bishop—not likely though, he didn't have a passel of kids.

Well, whoever this special farmer was, Marie loved him, because she loved the lunches at school. Especially the peanut butter sandwiches and homemade rolls. Rolls soft and warm like the tummy of her cat, but even better because you could eat them.

How Marie looked forward to Mondays. After a long weekend of lumpy mush—truly one of her greatest moments of joy was eating school lunch.

Chapter Fourteen

Marie thought nothing else could bring her the satisfaction those hot school lunches did. Now her tummy didn't grind and roll under her ribs at night, keeping her awake; it just felt a bit hungry because she hadn't eaten her mush. She hated it and now that she had something better, she preferred eating only once a day.

Not that she didn't get hungry—when lunchtime came she was mighty hungry! Only now it was a hunger she could at least sleep through. Marie was soon to find something that would feed her spirit bringing even more joy!

In some way that Marie could not comprehend, her lack of school lunch brought the Mormon Missionaries to teach her non-member stepfather about something called "the gospel." She overheard her mother muttering about it one night as she was preparing the corn meal mush.

Marie knew better than to outright question her, because she would clam up tighter than Patches' jaws when she wanted to feed him something he didn't want to eat.

So she almost held her breath as she stood very still behind her mother to listen as she was talking out loud to herself. "Maybe if it takes, maybe if he'll just listen and join the Mormon Church, we'll get some help. I never thought I'd want to take welfare but . . ."

Emma sighed deeply, something she did almost constantly now. "I told him he don't have to believe, just join. He's gonna do it, too! He's actually going to maybe join this church just to get welfare help. Maybe that ain't right, but God'll forgive me; I don't know what to do . . ."

Emma stood at the sink staring and sighing—nearly forgetting about the boiling water waiting for the mush. As she slowly scooped a portion of meal, she muttered to herself again.

"I don't know myself if this church is true." Just then she glanced up and her smile disappeared as she noticed Marie intently listening.

The missionaries came that night. When they knocked on the door, her mother was all a flurry, picking up the pot and dishes scattered about the room. She took off her apron, smoothed back her damp hair from her beautiful brow, and headed for the door. It didn't even occur to Marie, the babies, or her stepfather to help, although Antonio did pull himself up from his reclining position.

Then he tossed his cigarette onto the floor, squashed it with the tip of his boot, squiggled it some and then kicked it under the skirt of the battered couch leaving a charcoal spot, trailed with ashes, on the hardwood floor. He looked at it for a second and then clumped his size fourteen boot over it. He didn't bother to stand and shake their hand, instead he grunted a welcome and motioned for them to sit on the couch and chair opposite.

After introducing themselves, Brother Marshall and Brother Larsen awkwardly slipped out of their coats and draped them over the shabby furniture, then took their assigned places.

Marie noticed that one of them also had a very large

umbrella which he leaned against the chair, "It was strange," she thought, "because it wasn't raining at all."

Emma quietly slipped into the kitchen with the baby and little boys and motioned for Marie to follow, but she stayed put—she was immensely interested. She couldn't remember another time they had entertained anyone in their home, other than Italian relatives and never strangers. Especially strange brothers with different last names. She mulled that around in her mind and decided they must come from a divorced family like she did; her brothers, after all, were Giovannis, and she was a Rhinehart.

Then before her mother could stop her, Marie slipped behind the wood stove, slid her back down the wall in the tight spot and rested her chin on her tightly tucked up knees. With her head slightly tilted and her eyes wide, she had the best seat in the house.

After a few pleasantries, Antonio abruptly grunted to them that they might as well begin. They indicated that perhaps, they should wait for his wife to join them.

"Naw, what for—she's already one of you'n," meaning Mormons, of course.

"Well yes, but we thought perhaps she would like to join us anyway."

"Naw, she's got dishes to do."

He said it with such gruffness they were speechless for a time. The one that called himself Brother Marshall shifted uncomfortably in the old recliner, placing his weight on his elbow and sitting forward quite a bit. Marie smiled to herself, at the same time feeling sorry for him because she knew the big spring in the chair without much stuffing over it, was pinching him unmercifully.

Seeing that Antonio didn't intend to invite his wife

back, Brother Larsen cleared his throat and began. He took his umbrella onto his lap and unsnapped the top of it.

Antonio wiped his brow and shifted around on the couch. Marie knew it was because he needed a cigarette, but she could tell he was pretty interested too, although she knew he wouldn't let the missionaries know that.

She noticed Brother Marshall squirming again and his look seemed to say, "Boy is this guy a loser; what a waste of time this is."

He was clearly uncomfortable looking directly at Antonio; his eyes wandered about the room as though searching for something to focus on, until they rested on the deer head. The brother called Marshall and that deer head spent much of the rest of the evening staring at each other.

Brother Larsen seemed oblivious to the discomfort as he pulled what looked to Marie like a large flannel diaper out of his umbrella case. She couldn't have been more fascinated had he been about to put on a magic show!

He unrolled the flannel, which now looked like the bamboo calendars with dowels in each end, that Aunt Kate always sent for Christmas. Then he poked some wires into the back that bowed and made the flannel stiff, while another set of wires hung straight down and acted like an easel to make the thing stand up. He then stood it teetering a little, on the old vinyl chair, facing toward Antonio.

Both Marie and Antonio were wide-eyed, almost waiting for a rabbit to be pulled from his strange umbrella case next. Instead, Brother Larsen pulled an envelope out of his coat pocket. Marie nearly chuckled out loud as she finally realized what he was doing. Out of the envelope came flannel board figures! As he placed them on the flannel board,

Marie was grateful that with a little more angle on her tilted head she could see just fine.

He began to teach them of something called a "Falling Away" and a "Restoration" and told the Joseph Smith story—just like Sharon had! Marie found this immensely interesting, but nothing could have compared to the story they told a few weeks later of the "Plan of Salvation."

That week started as they usually did, with her mother in the other room and Marie in the corner behind the wood stove. The missionary told how we had all lived before in the pre-something Marie couldn't remember that word but we had lived there with a Heavenly Father.

Antonio was even more squirmy this week for his cigarettes, and Marie noticed he didn't seem as interested. He was becoming more and more impatient with these preachers coming to interrupt his T.V. programs, and Marie could sense that he felt like they were judging him. She could guess his mind was thinking that all this religion might not be worth the welfare, after all. He took out his big, dingy handkerchief, wiped his brow, noisily blew his nose on it and stuffed it back into his pocket with most of it hanging out.

The missionaries went on to teach that Heavenly Father was God, and He was kind and loved us and wanted us to go back home to Him. He said we came here on earth for a test and that if we passed we could go back to Heaven. And that after we died we would get our bodies back in a ressur-something.

"They mean Grandpa Daddy will come back!" Marie thought, as her heart began filling with joy. She was mesmerized as the missionary placed circles on the flannel board representing the kingdoms we could go to after this life.

She couldn't pronounce the names—"T" something but she was profoundly impressed with the fact that one would be the home of the very bad people, like murderers. One was for pretty good people and the last was for the very righteous, the very best people—the ones who got A's on their test of life!

As Brother Larsen's story unfolded something happened to Marie. She began to feel a burning in her heart and it spread over her whole body. She could never remember feeling this warm, good feeling before in her life. It started her tears and they poured down her face, over her chin and continued in rivers down her skinny unwashed legs.

A voice seemed to be saying in her head, "This is true, this is all true!" Her young eleven-year-old mind had grasped and understood the principles being taught and she accepted them with all her heart.

Suddenly Antonio stood up, right in the middle of the discussion and reached into his back pocket. He pulled out his cigarettes and matches, sat back down, and lit one taking a good long draw on it. The missionaries forgot to hide their shock and disapproval.

"So cut the bull!"

Antonio went on to swear and curse, telling the missionaries that he knew they didn't approve of a man who smoked. Well, he wouldn't have them coming into his home anymore, judging him. Who were they to tell him he was going to hell, anyway?

With their mouths agape, and as quickly as possible, they gathered up their things. They stuffed the cutouts into the envelope, rolled up the flannel board and without even stuffing it back into it's case, they threw their coats over their arms and left. Marie imagined them pulling on their coats, out in the cold, as they hurried away. Then she looked up to see her angry stepfather staring directly into her big frightened eyes!

Marie had thought she might quit breathing as she shoved her face into her pillow, trying desperately to smother her sobs. As frightened as she was of bringing her stepfather's wrath down on her again, she couldn't stop the sobbing.

Much later in the dark, dark of that night, Marie lay huddled in her bed—still shuddering from her long bout of sobbing. She breathed deeply, shuddered, then breathed deeply again, over and over until she calmed down and lay still.

She winced as her sore ear rubbed the pillow and rolled to her other side. Still her eyes would not close in sleep. Over and over in her mind she played the scenes of that night.

Her stepfather rarely hit her; he hurt her with ugly words constantly, but rarely with physical violence. When he did, he always went for the ears. He always boxed ears! She was glad though, because her hair would cover her bruised and swollen ear—she didn't want to explain that to anyone.

For a while her heart dwelled on blackness; she was certain that he would go to the bad place, "T" somcthing. As she sobbed and sobbed she felt glad that he would go to that bad place.

After the sobbing subsided her calmer thoughts turned to the things the strange brothers had said. She was sorry they wouldn't be coming back again. She'd hoped they would explain what a Jack Mormon was. But she remembered every detail of what they did teach; it was etched on her mind like a photograph.

For the rest of her life, Marie would be able to close her eyes and conjure up that flannel board. With the image in her mind of the three degrees of glory would come that wonderful feeling of peace and she could feel the voice again in her heart saying, "It's true!"

As her thoughts turned to these things, she felt a wonderful peace. A feeling of joy she had never known began to engulf and enfold her. She felt safe and protected and no longer afraid. She felt strangely almost lifted from the bed as the darkness in the room gave way to a wonderful glowing light. A light she could not see with her natural eyes, but in her mind's eye. A bright, white, glowing, moving light, circling and circling and circling . . .

Chapter Fifteen

Marie walked around the side of the school, farthest from the playground and sat on the hard, cold ground. Leaning against the building, she pulled her thin coat up over her head and close about her face. For once she was glad it was too big.

The sounds of the other children in the school seemed muffled and far away. She looked up into the vast grey sky, heavy with an approaching storm. Her eyes wandered to the barren trees and shrubs. It should have been a day guaranteed to make her depressed; quite often the lack of sunlight did get Marie down, but not today.

Today the grey sky and barren earth were beautiful beyond compare. They were beautiful in a way she had never known before. They were beautiful because suddenly Marie knew in her heart that they were here for a reason. The snow would come and water the thirsty ground. The cold would store it safely until spring sunshine would melt it, sending it rushing down streams and canals to water the farmers' crops and the big trees and green, green grass and most of all the flowers!

Without having actually been taught by mortal man, Marie was now being taught these truths. Her young mind was not too immature to comprehend that all this had been created for her and all the other people—wherever they were in the whole world.

The light that had seemed to encircle her all the night long, was still with her. Her joy was so full it seemed her heart would explode! Her complete soul seemed to commune with her Heavenly Father. Having only prayed once in her entire life, her heart was drawn out now in prayer and thanksgiving to Heaven.

All the loneliness, all the heartache she had ever endured seemed swallowed up in this wonderful knowledge and joy. In a way that she could not comprehend, she knew that in those moments, all was well with the world—her world. She had never felt such security and well being before; she had never felt so cherished and beloved.

Many dark days would come to the life of this small child, crouched alone in a school yard. There would be many, many times when sorrow and unhappiness would engulf her soul until she would hardly remember this moment of total peace and security, yet she would never be the same. For all the days of her life, she would have this anchor to her soul.

This knowledge she was endowed with; would be as a shining star to her, forever. It would be to her a guiding light, and when she would look to it, inevitably the clouds of darkness would always clear. The sun would always come out again!

Marie looked across the street at Mr. Hansen's store. Kind Mr. Hansen, did he have this wonderful knowing? He must, for how else could he have such heavenly blue angel eyes!

She looked at Mrs. Jemison's house right next door. Did she know these wonderful things too? Surely she must—else how could she show such love for a poor child.

Then Marie's eyes wandered to Mrs. Botti's house. Now there was someone who surely did not know. Marie was all ready to bristle in her mind at the thought of that fat, coffee-drinking woman who was probably a witch, when the strangest thing happened. A voice in her head seemed to say that she was also loved by Heavenly Father—that he loves all people, for they are his children.

Her mind could not for the life of her think ill of anyone at this moment. Without knowing why, she felt suddenly drawn to Mrs. Botti's house—to her, and she knew in some inexplicable way that their paths would cross again. It did not frighten her or worry her in the least. "How strange," she thought.

Marie was startled out of her pondering by the shrill sound of the bell calling her back to earth and school. As she scrambled up, she glanced at the church on the other side of Mr. Hansen's store. With that glance came another sharp impression, that she needed to attend Primary.

The thought brought her a moment of fear. Every Tuesday afternoon school was dismissed one half hour early and all the children, except Marie, would run across the street to Primary. Mrs. Jemison and Sharon had invited her to come, but she always declined, and headed for home. The last thing in the world she needed was to spend more humiliating time with the boys of Walker, and she wasn't even sure just what Primary was.

She suspected that it was like Catholic Catechism. Her step grandmother had insisted that she attend with the Catholic children in their old neighborhood. Marie went willingly, and with a great deal of curiosity, which soon changed to fear and dread.

The inside of the Catholic Church was so dark and

silent; no child would dare make a sound. The great ladies dressed in black were stern and forbidding and they taught about a mysterious God and a terrible place, where all wicked go called Limbo. The children were made to learn monotonous chants that seemed like gobbeldygoop to Marie.

No, she wasn't being forced to go to Primary here, and was happy to stay away—thank you! Still the impression that she must attend Primary was very strong and real; she wondered about it the rest of that school day.

The Lord and his angels in Heaven are not asleep on their job, for no sooner had they enlightened and softened the heart of little Marie Rhinehart, than they provided her an opportunity to act on her impression. This very day was Tuesday, and as she was about to leave school, she felt drawn again to the large church across the street.

She stood there, looking and wondering just outside the door. She seemed lost in another world as the other children, totally oblivious of her, headed boisterously across the street.

"Marie."

Mrs. Jemison called her name again, "Marie." Still Marie did not respond, so she walked closer and gently laid her hand on her shoulder. Marie jumped then and quickly gathered her things to bolt for home.

"Marie, would you like to join us in Primary today?"

Try as she might to object, the angels must have bound her tongue, for not a word would come out.

Taking this as encouragement, Mrs. Jemison again extended her invitation. "You're welcome to come—why don't you join us today?" Then as an afterthought she added, "Will your mother worry if you aren't home right after school?"

"No, I usually play around a lot after school. She doesn't ever notice."

"Well it's all settled then; come along!"

With that Mrs. Jemison put her arm around her young charge and steered her in the direction of the church. Marie found herself propelled into the large three-story dark brick building.

Inside the overcast day made it dark and she fully expected to see the great dark Nuns swoop down on her like in the Catholic Church—but she saw no such thing. Instead Mrs. Jemison steered her to a bench and seated her next to Sharon. Sharon gave her a big, big grin, which helped a lot!

A woman Marie didn't know stood at the podium and welcomed all the children to Primary.

"That's my mother! She's a counselor in the Primary Presidency," Sharon whispered.

That sounded important to Marie and she looked with curiosity at this woman who was very important and had forbade her daughter to befriend Marie.

As Sharon's mother spoke to the children, Mrs. Jemison, who was seated on the stand behind her, stood up and whispered something in her ear.

She reluctantly looked out at the children and then into the face of Marie. "Ah, we—seem to have someone new in Primary today. Miss Rhinehart, would you like to stand?"

No! No, she would not like to stand! Her face went beet red and all the boys began to guffaw and laugh at her. Sharon gave her a push and she slowly stood. Her face was pale and she was frightened out of her wits; she could not have felt worse if she had been on trial for her life!

She stood and stood, not knowing why she needed to,

or what to expect, until Sharon's *important* mom thanked her and told her she could sit down now. The boys laughed again and Marie had to fight hard to keep her tears back. Then they promptly forgot her and listened to some talks by kids in her school.

"I would die if they made me do that!" thought Marie. "I will definitely never come again if they try!"

Then they sang some songs. The songs were wonderful! They put Marie at ease, and even though she didn't know them and could barely join in, she listened and felt the music soothe her soul. Then it was time to dismiss for classes.

Sharon motioned for her to follow, "Come on, Marie, we're in Sister Pickering's class."

Off they went with tiny, petite old Sister Pickering. She was so old she went very slowly, but Marie noticed she didn't shuffle like some old people, or seem awkward in any way. She was very graceful. Marie thought instantly that she was beautiful. Strange, she had never thought of anyone old, as beautiful before—well, except maybe Mr. Hansen, if men could be beautiful.

There they were together, all five sixth graders: Sharon, Joan, Mike, that awful Jack Carlson and herself. He gave her a big grin, meaning he was ready for anything and she could just as well plan on it. She sat as far away from him as possible, and looked warily around the room, wondering if her chair was booby trapped.

"This should be awful," thought Marie. Jack Carlson was a loud-mouthed obnoxious kid if ever there was one. She had never seen Jack Carlson sit still. But today he did. Marie soon found out why.

She was amazed when Sister Pickering began to teach.

Her voice was tiny and quiet, and although it was old like her walk, it was steady and fervent. And Sister Pickering had fire in her eyes! Not a fire that would ever scare anyone, except maybe the very, very wicked, Marie thought, but a fire that was alive—alive with a testimony of the gospel of Jesus Christ.

"Why," thought Marie, "she knows this great truth too!" This was even better than being taught by the missionaries! Marie's soul was like a sponge and she drank and drank and drank at these wonderful waters of truth! The teacher was ever so kind to her and invited her to come back. Why had she waited so long to come? Marie knew she would never miss again!

It felt so good she lingered until all the children had filed out. Finding herself alone with kind Sister Pickering, she blurted out the one question that no one had answered, "Could you tell me please, what is a Jack Mormon?"

Sister Pickering seemed surprised and replied, "There's really no such thing."

"But, Jack Carlson says I'm one."

"Well, he's wrong, because that's just an old saying for someone who is a Mormon, but doesn't come to church."

"I haven't been to church before, so I guess I am one."

"You came today, so I guess you're not, are you?" Sister Pickering said with a big smile. She gave Marie a hug and invited her back again.

What a relief! It wasn't as bad as all that. Why did the boys and Joan say "Jack Mormon" with such terrible insinuations? They must not know that some people just don't understand they should go to church. She was so glad to understand that "Jack Mormon" didn't mean "Bad Mormon" just a lost one—a lost lamb who had just been found.

She left with that wonderful feeling of being surrounded by light, the white encircling light of the gospel, the light of truth, the light of Christ!

On the way out she passed right by Sharon's mom Sister Pace, they called her. Strange—maybe everyone in this town was related, all brothers and sisters. Who could have that many children? Well, there were too many mysteries for her young mind, so she put that one away. She could feel that Sister Pace did not approve of her as she mumbled that she was glad Marie had come. Her words were right, but her heart wasn't, and Marie could feel every bit of it.

With a little of the air punched out of her bubble she started for home, when she heard someone calling.

"Hey, Marie, wait up for me!"

Marie turned around to see Sharon puffing up behind her.

"Marie, wait I wanna' talk to ya'. I saw you leave Primary—an' I saw how my mom was." Sharon seemed a little embarrassed, but felt a need to apologize to Marie and try to explain her mother's actions. She didn't know quite how to say it so she blurted, "You know I love her anyway?"

Marie could only nod. Of course she knew that Marie loved her mom. She could only conclude that there was something innately wrong with herself and that was why Sister Pace treated her so coldly. But Marie was certain that Sharon's attitude was suggesting her mom was wrong!

"See Marie, I just don't think my mom understands. I can't explain it really, but—do you know what I mean?"

Marie didn't, but she nodded anyway and gave her friend a great big smile!

"Good. I knew you'd understand!"

She didn't understand Sharon's mother, but she did understand Sharon—she was the *best* friend in the world.

With her bubble re-inflated Marie stood in the road smiling and waving as Sharon, with her long, dark hair flying behind, ran to her mother's station wagon.

Feeling good again, she turned around to head for home and saw petite Sister Pickering just disappearing into Hansen's store. The door was heavy and she was laden with Primary supplies and books. The top book flew off into the snow.

Marie rushed to her side and picked up the book, wiping the wet snow off before she handed it back.

She noticed that the book was very worn and the pages seemed puffed out, almost like the tissue flowers they had made in school last year. For a moment Marie wondered if the snow had damaged it, but quickly realized that was impossible.

Sister Pickering thanked Marie as she reached out for her Book of Mormon—the book with onion skin paper, marked and swollen from hours of feasting upon the word. Had Marie and Sharon asked Sister Pickering why Sharon's mom didn't understand, she would have directed them to read Alma 5:14: *"And now behold, I ask of you, my brethren of the church, have ye spiritually been born of God? Have ye received his image in your countenances? Have ye experienced this mighty change in your hearts?"*

But Sister Pickering *did* pass on the Christ-like love in her heart to Marie by warming her with a smile of gratitude as she pushed through the store door.

Marie turned toward home again. All the way there she marveled again at all that had happened to her in such a short time.

She pondered what Sharon had said about her mother and she realized something important. This knowledge of the truth—this kind of understanding, didn't come because of age. She suddenly understood that even Mr. Adams, as old as he was, or Jack Carlson as young as he was, probably didn't understand these things either—and they were *all* baptized Mormons!

It was one thing to have someone tell you the story of Joseph Smith and an angel and gold plates. That was a nice story and all, but it was quite something else to *know for yourself* that it was all very much the truth—and she did!

As she thought of all this again on the way home, her bubble grew and grew and with it came a magnanimous generosity for all the mean things that had ever been meted out to her in life. At this rate she could even like the old Grandma Giovanni.

Well, she wouldn't stretch things by thinking too hard on that!

Chapter Sixteen

No one can gain a testimony of the truth and not want to share it with the world! Marie felt even more happy about this than the birth of her little sister. She wanted to have a party and invite all the world to come hear the good news!

Thereafter, every relative she had would hear a fervent testimony from this young girl. For all the years she would live with them, every aunt, uncle, cousin, mother and brother would hear from Marie as many times as occasion would permit, that the gospel was true. She went about bearing testimony of the truthfulness of the Book of Mormon! A book she had not yet seen—let alone read!

Her mother was regaled with stories from Primary each week. Her stepfather's sister-in-law moved into the nearest town—just twenty miles away, and Marie went sometimes to babysit for them. Once she spent the night with her Step-Aunt, Josephine, because her husband was out of town. Marie kept her up until the wee hours of the morning, telling all that she had learned from the missionaries and Sharon and Primary!

The woman listened with awe and respect all the night long. And many would be the times of death or tragedy in the family that these same adults would turn to the girl in her youth for comfort and understanding. Her great faith seemed to sustain and carry them all. Even so, her labors seemed in vain for not one ever became active members of Christ's true church. Yet all looked to her for comfort in time of need. All except her stepfather.

This new found faith in such a young thing excited his desire to persecute her even further. The girl had always infuriated him. Her complete acceptance of the same missionaries he had himself rejected could not have rubbed him more wrong.

"Miss Goody Two Shoes" and "Miss Molly Mormon" and "Don't She Think She's Somethin'" and "Holier Than Thou" were labels he constantly lashed out at her.

It was already well-established that the best way to get her goat was to humiliate her mother. The man simply could not resist the temptation now to get her to lose her temper—and lose it Marie did. She would fall into his trap so often and feel so bad afterward as he laughed his hideous laugh of triumph! The situation at home was getting increasingly tense and poor Emma was caught in the middle of it all.

"It is strange," thought Marie, "because I have *not* tried to share these things with my stepfather—not once." In fact he was the only one she could think of she hadn't shared them with, yet he hated her just because he knew she believed!

It was these events, more than anything, that led to the next episode in Marie's life. Marie became even more adept at compartmentalizing her life. She had a tense and miserable home life. She had an intense and exhilarating missionary life. And she had school.

School right now consisted of the Christmas Pageant and the fact that she would dance. Marie couldn't have wanted this more than a girl who longs for the day she will marry the man she loves! After finding out all about the pre-existence she immediately decided that she had danced her way through that existence. It felt better than breathing.

Sometimes she could still meet Sharon in their special place down by the bridge to play. But for some reason her attendance at Primary, instead of softening the heart of Sharon's mother, seemed to increase her resolve to keep her daughter away from this strange child and her heathen family.

Because her life at home was so bad, Marie spent most of her time, after school and on weekends, outdoors. Her mother did not object, probably finding relief from the discord in her absence. She played in the sheds with Patches and down by the bridge, and still climbed the stark barren trees to read in, but mostly she spent her time dancing—dancing on her wonderful stage in the reeds.

Just before the whole creek froze over someone had damned up part of the creek upstream, for whatever reason she did not know. At first she was heartbroken because the waters had flooded over into her stage in the reeds. But as the thin layer of water froze, it made a nice little frozen pond.

Oh, how she would dearly love to have a pair of ice skates, but no matter, her shoes were so worn and slippery they made wonderful makeshift skates. There for hours and hours she would slide and glide and practice the steps to her dance. Never had anyone been more prepared for a performance.

It was on one such Saturday afternoon when Marie was dancing her heart out, lost in her world of make believe like only Marie could be, that it happened. She would reproach herself for many days for not hearing them come; she should have heard them coming. She should have heard their big dumb dog barking.

Oh, when would she learn to pay more attention. The first thing she knew she found herself sprawled on the ice with that monster shaggy dog of Jack Carlson's nearly on top of her, barking his head off. His big paw was on the sleeve of her coat and he was so close she could smell his awful, slobbery dog breath and feel its warmth on her face in gusts, as he barked.

Big dogs scared her to death anyway. Once in first grade she was late for school and took a shortcut through an alley. A dog, as large and muscled as a horse, leaped out, snarling and snapping at her. Straining at the end of a big metal chain, he stopped short of her face by a fraction of an inch. She was so frightened she stood rooted to the spot for what seemed like an eternity; finally she made herself back up and ran crying for her mother.

She would be terrified of big dogs the rest of her life. So when Jack's dog jumped on her, she nearly fainted from a terrifying fright, until the laughing boy and his brothers finally called the dog off.

"Serves ya right! What were you doin' in the reeds anyway?" laughed one of the boys.

"Looked to me like *EDNA* was trying to fly, like a dumb bird," laughed another, as they turned with their dog in tow, and without a glance back, left the sobbing Marie sprawled on the ice.

She had been so frightened she hadn't noticed the terrible throbbing pain in her leg. She realized that during the fall she had slammed it hard into a left over iron fence pole sticking up near the edge of the pond. After she quit trembling so hard, she sat up and tried to stand. She screamed in pain as she tried to put weight on her leg and fell back down.

Just then her little brother, Tony, who normally didn't stray so far from home came through the reeds. "Wha'sa matter, Marie?" He asked in sincere concern. "Are ya hurt?"

Marie, through her tears, told him to run get mamma and he scuttled away on his chubby little legs for home.

Chapter Seventeen

Marie sobbed into the crisply starched pillow that smelled of fresh air and flowers in the spring. She kept wondering how her mother could have done this to her. Her throbbing leg, set so stiffly in a cast from the top of her leg to the tip of her toes, was a grim reminder of her dashed dreams.

"As if that isn't enough," she punched at the sweet crisp pillow and pushed her face into it deeper, lamenting, "How could my mother do this—how could she!" Then feeling guilty for crying all over the lovely thing, she sobbed even harder.

Suddenly startled by a large warm hand on her forehead, she jerked away. "Vot, little von. Do not cry so 'til it will break my very heart. Is it the pain? Do you need some pain-killers?"

"No."

Marie shrank even farther away and buried her face into the pillow again, refusing to be comforted. How could this woman know that she was as much distressed about being here as about her leg hurting? How could her mother have done this to her?

Mrs. Bottigheimer, sensing that Marie was in no mood to be comforted said, "You sleep, little von, just try to sleep, ve'll talk in the morning." Then quietly she left the room.

How much more horrible could one day get than this one had been. After little Tony brought help, her mother and stepfather had loaded her into their ram-shackle car and driven her the twenty miles to the hospital again. Only this time she was aware of every bump and rut in the road, as well as every comment from her parents that came with as much sharp hurt. All the way there she was made to understand just how much this one would cost. Surely the family would never eat again and all because of her carelessness! Then came the pain of having her leg x-rayed and set and the miserable ride home, followed by the fight between her parents after she was tucked into bed with a pain pill.

Marie had finally drifted off to sleep just in time to be awakened by her mother who was hustling around her room, shoving a few of her belongings into a paper bag. "Mamma, what are you doing?" Her mother just tossed Marie her coat and told her to quickly put it on.

"Where are we going?"

Without a word her mother tossed aside the blankets and covered her bare toes with a warm sock, scooped Marie up in her arms, and headed for the door. Outside they climbed into the truck and drove down the lane to town. Marie could not get a word out of her mother and so resigned herself to silence, but could not imagine what her mother was doing.

The truck stopped in front of the Witch Woman's door!

Emma was not a large woman and her child was nearly twelve; yet she seemed to summon great reserves of strength from adrenaline and determination as she hoisted Marie into her arms again, and carried her right up to Mrs. Botti's door. Marie was so astonished she was speechless!

At the door, Emma explained that she needed help and Berta ushered them in. The next thing Marie knew her mother had deposited her in the large brass bed she had been in last time she was in this gingerbread house. After talking in the other room with Mrs. Botti for some time, without another word to Marie, she left—left her behind!

Marie had never felt so abandoned and confused in her life. Mrs. Botti was very kind and solicitous as she tried to explain that Marie would only be here for a few weeks, until she could get used to her cast and get around on crutches. When she was well enough to go back to school, she could go home.

Marie spoke not a word, but simply stared in unbelief and looked like one stricken. Mrs. Botti left her then and came back in a while with a nice warm bowl of delicious stew, piping hot rolls and a large glass of warm milk. She wanted so badly for the "little von" as she called her, to talk with her, but Marie maintained her silence and just picked at the wonderful dinner. Afterward she rolled over and commenced crying into her pillow.

Marie had been given a few horrible surprises in her life—her mother never told her anything—but this took the cake. She would never, ever forgive her for this one. She imagined that if she became dinner for this witch—dinner delivered by her own mother, it would serve her right if she were sad about it the rest of her life. Her last conscious thought before she fell into a troubled sleep was her hope that her mother would mourn forever for what she had done.

Her leg was caught in something, she tugged and pulled and struggled to pull it free. It was time to go on the stage, the crowd was calling for her. "Ma-rie, Ma-rie," they chanted, calling for her to thrill them with her wondrous dance.

The struggle made her leg hurt, it throbbed and ached. She tossed this way and that—and all around her it was dark. Then out of the darkness came an enormously fat woman. She was so big she filled the horizon until she blotted out the sun. She was so big Marie felt like an insect, loathsome and unwanted.

Marie nearly screamed as she came closer, certain that her gigantic fat foot would squash her flat. As she came nearer her flabby arm reached down from miles above the earth. Marie flinched and moved aside as she began taking her toys away—first her dolls, then her stove and then she put her ironing board down a deep, deep cleft on the cold dark mountain, where Marie's throbbing leg held her prisoner.

"No—not that. You can't hide it from me!" Marie screamed out from her bed.

Her screams woke her and it took a few moments for her pounding heart to subside and her conscious mind to register where she was.

"Vat, there now child. You've had a nightmare!" Mrs. Bottigheimer rushed into the room to comfort the screaming child. She picked Marie up out of the bed and carried her to the rocking chair in the corner. She cradled the gangly eleven-year-old on her lap and rocked and crooned sweet comfort.

In spite of her fear of this stranger, young Marie, hungry for love succumbed to the comfort and snuggled into the softness of Mrs. Botti's large bosom. Frightened by her dream, bewildered by her mother's abandonment, and now more hurt by her throbbing leg—a poignant reminder that she would not dance in the pageant, Marie began to cry.

Since she had broken her leg she would not allow herself to feel the hurt and pain of the realization that her one dream in life was gone. If Mrs. Botti had been harsh, or unfeeling, or had even ignored her as her mother usually did, perhaps she could have kept her numb walls of protection up. But as she lay cuddled in the incredibly comforting bosom of this woman, her pain rose to the surface.

A pain that had little to do with the ache in her broken leg seemed to crush her chest with great force. A pain indistinguishable between the disappointment of not dancing, and the bewildering and frightening abandonment of her mother, swirled in her heart like a cold chocolate and vanilla ice cream twist.

It came in waves of sorrow that made her make a groaning sound between her silent tears. Marie was no stranger to disappointment; this hurt more than her mother's marriage to a strange man, more than losing her toys, more than their move, more than the boys teasing, more than her humiliation at being poor, even more than her rejection by Sharon's mother. It *almost* hurt as much as losing Grandpa Daddy!

The realization of this brought with it a depression she had never known. In all of her almost twelve years of life, after each disappointing moment, she had always squared her shoulders and gone on. She had become very adept at stuffing the disappointment away quickly, with an incredible acceptance of her harsh life—it was, after all, as it always was.

This time she felt so betrayed that she could not stuff the pain away—she just felt as though she could not go on. She determined never to let anything or anyone become this important to her again. No amount of joy or anticipation could compensate for this pain of loss.

Marie of course did not know how to express any of this, so she simply lay moaning and weeping her silent tears, sheltered in Mrs. Botti's arms. She cried until the rocking of the chair finally lulled her back to sleep—safe, sweet, comforting sleep.

Mrs. Bottigheimer gently laid her in bed, her heart more than a little sore for the anguish she felt from this little von as she called her. She marveled that one so young could feel such pain and sorrow, for her very spirit could feel this was no childish, momentary fright, but real and deep anguish.

Marie slept then, on through the evening—on through the night, but Mrs. Bottigheimer slept fitfully. Her mind ran around and around for ideas to take away the hurt and bring some joy into Marie's young life. Meanwhile, since sleep was so elusive she got up and lumbered to her clay table in the other room, where she began molding a new doll face.

Chapter Eighteen

Lacy white and lightly frosted with ice and snow, the tree outside the window looked like something in a picture book. The sun filtered through the lace from a crisp blue sky, and in spite of herself, Marie felt much better. She lay there drinking in its beauty until Mrs. Botti peeked her chubby face around the corner with a smile.

Despite her previous fears, Marie no longer felt frightened. Through all her confusion and sorrow and even rudeness yesterday, Mrs. Botti's kind, compassionate nature had shone through. The words her Primary teacher read to the children from the Bible swam around in her head—something like, "I was a stranger and ye took me in." Marie was a stranger and Mrs. Botti had taken her in.

"Well, now how do you feel, little von, better, ja?"

Marie stared at her for a moment and shyly said, "Uh-huh."

"Good." And with that she swept from the door and was back in an instant, with the most amazing breakfast tray Marie had ever beheld. Bacon, eggs, pancakes, marmalade, syrup, milk and juice! It was even bigger than the breakfast Antonio's Mamma had made for him.

With large round eyes and not another word she began to eat. She ate until her tummy hurt, still she could not quit eating. Nothing had ever tasted so good. While Marie ate,

Mrs. Botti pulled up a chair and watched with pleasure as the child devoured her food. Mrs. Botti pulled a tiny doll garment from her pocket and began to stitch.

"A good cook always enjoys watching her food disappear," Mrs. Bottigheimer said with an enormously pleased smile. Then, in happy, companionable silence, she stitched away while the child ate. After she finished, Mrs. Botti cleared away the dishes, bustled in the kitchen for a short time cleaning up, and then reappeared.

She pulled her chair up close to Marie and said, "This time we need to have a chat, just you and me child."

Marie felt a little apprehensive but let her do the talking.

"Why are you afraid of me?"

Marie just shrugged her shoulders.

"Perhaps the other little vons have told you I was a witch?"

Marie wouldn't respond, but her eyes got larger.

"Yes, I can see that it is so. Well I am certainly not a witch. I am just a lonely old woman, who really loves children. I am sorry that I have scared all the people of this place. You see, I think that they are worried about me because I am not a Mormon, ja?"

Marie could not help but nod her head in the affirmative. "If the truth be told, I have not been too friendly with these Mormons. All these brothers and sisters, they seemed to love my Branca, but I have no use for Mormons! But, well, let me tell you what I am, so you do not be afraid anymore, since you must stay in my home for a few veeks, ja."

Mrs. Botti went on to tell her a story that made Marie cry. Berta Bottigheimer had all the time in the world—with the day stretching out as long as each day in its turn had done before, for so many years. Yet today she had a captive audience, a young girl in bed with an enormous white cast on a little skinny leg.

She told Marie of her wonderful and happy childhood. Of her great large family of nine brothers and one sister and her wonderful parents. She described their attractive little home in Amsterdam Holland—an enchanting city of tiny islands, and her lovely attic bedroom that she shared with her only sister.

Her sister Branca was only a year older than she, and she couldn't have loved anyone more. They shared everything—clothes, friends, books, a bedroom and, most of all, their hearts! Berta could hardly remember when they had even quarreled and each night before they went to sleep they would whisper into the dark, "I love you Berta," and "I love you too Branca."

In fact the girls were so close they didn't even have room in their lives for young men. Their mother despaired of ever having them marry, and at the ripe old age of twenty four and twenty five they were considered "Old Maids." Berta could never conceive of a world without her Branca and as she continued her story, she had to reach for her handkerchief and noisily relieve her stuffy nose.

Marie could feel the resentment oozing from her every pore as she went on to tell of how a young American came into Branca's life and bewitched her. Always they had shared everything and Branca had loved her best, until Frank Jorgensen had come along. He had come to visit his relatives after spending two years in England. He left with Branca's heart.

Her parents liked him well enough, and although he

was an American, he had a good family from Holland. They knew of his grandparents and heartily approved.

One day shortly after he left, two strange young Americans showed up at their door. They had been sent by Frank and were part of a strange American cult—the "Mormons!" Branca's parents were aghast, for she had not told them that the Frank they had admired so, had been a Mormon! They had no idea that that was the reason he'd been in England—he was a missionary too!

They forbade the missionaries to ever come back and forbade Branca to ever write Frank Jorgensen again! Branca confided in Berta, however, that she continued to see the missionaries and to write to Frank behind their parents back. She had always been such an obedient and faithful daughter, and it broke Berta's heart to see her do this. She kept Branca's confidence, for she loved her so, but she almost never forgave her for not telling her of her plan to join Frank in America.

After Branca left, Berta cried into her pillow every night for months. How could she leave and not even tell her beloved sister? Later Branca wrote and told her she hadn't dared reveal her plan, even to Berta, for fear she would panic and tell her parents.

Berta tried to understand, but she felt bitter instead. Her parents disowned her beloved sister and sent her letters back marked "Return to Sender." Berta could not do this and so she opened a post office box to receive Branca's mail, until World War II broke out.

Berta soon found herself also in love with a wonderful young man from across town. She had known him in school and despised him for a little hooligan. She hadn't seen him since grade school and was amazed at the change in him when she met him again at his father's lace factory, where she worked.

Albert Bottigheimer's family had moved to Amsterdam from Ghent Belgium during World War I. They fled the invasion of Germany in 1914 and set up their lace making industry near Berta's home. Since she had known him in school, Albert had grown so tall and handsome and mannerly. He didn't pull her braids anymore, but stole her heart instead.

A few days before he left for war, he asked Berta's father for her hand in marriage, which he heartily gave! They were married the next day, quietly at home, and had only two blessed days together before he left. As the mail could get through, she wrote to him all the years of that long, horrible war. Their love increased and they made plans for their wonderful happy future together.

Berta had to stop then and go into the bathroom to mop her face and blow her nose. She then told of that morning so long ago when she had gone to the train station—the whole city had turned out to welcome the returning soldiers. In vain she scoured the faces and lines of young men returning in such joyful reunions with loved ones. She waited until the last train load of young men had been deposited and in disappointment turned to go home, certain that he would be on the train tomorrow.

As she left a young man took her shoulder. As she turned around he glanced down at a photograph he held in his hands and then back at her. Seeming to be satisfied, he asked if she were Berta Bottigheimer?

"Yes."

"I—I have some awful news for you."

Berta wiped her tears and reached into the nightstand

drawer to pull out a very worn old book. Marie noticed the title as she pulled it to her ample bosom and held it there. It was *Grimm's Fairy Tales*! What in the world, Marie wondered?

Berta told Marie how her young husband had been killed in the last battle of the war. The day before he had a premonition that he would not be going home and gave all his possessions to his best friend. He asked him to find Berta and give them to her, along with a letter. Berta pulled that fragile yellowed letter out of her book and translated, as she read it to Marie.

"My Dear Beloved Berta,

"I feel that I will not be coming home to you. My heart wants to break for the sorrow that you will feel. Berta if my spirit lives on I will watch over you forever from heaven and God willing we will meet again there someday. I will be waiting with outstretched arms.

"Berta I want you to have a book that my granny gave to me. It might seem kind of funny to you, but granny loved fairy tales. When I was a little kid she told me that I must believe in them. Oh, not that the stories really happened, but she wanted me to believe in the message found in them. That message was one of hope!

"In fairy tales, the good guys always win over evil. Cinderella always finds her prince (and you found me, right?) And the bewitched good prince is always restored, no matter the evil that is done to him.

"Ah, Gran could spin a yarn. She was

famous throughout the entire country-side for her storytelling. I can remember so many cold winter nights, huddled together with my brothers and cousins near Granny's warm fire. The room would disappear as she carried us into her world of make-believe! Granny wanted me to be good and she wanted me to remember that, as she always said, "Right Makes Might!" She always quoted me her favorite scripture from Romans 8:28, "And we know that all things work together for good to them that love God." She really believed that—she had such faith!

"She also taught me that Fairy Godmothers only grant make believe-wishes in stories, but Jesus Christ is real! He is the only one who truly transforms evil into good, sorrow into joy, death into life.

"Berta, tomorrow I fear, I will be turned into dust, but God willing, just as His son Jesus Christ was, I will be changed someday into a living man again. Berta, be good, and my little Cinderella, I will hold you again in my arms, just believe Berta—believe in the message of hope found in fairy tales and be good.

"Until I am transformed again in Christ, forever your frog prince.

All My Love, Al"

Berta handed Marie a handkerchief and both cried for sometime. Marie had never heard a more wonderful or tragic or romantic story before in her life.

She remembered the book Berta had given her and how

she had tossed it into the corner, uncaring and disgusted. Marie truly hoped her book was safe and she knew that she would treasure it now. She knew she would read it from cover to cover! Finally she blew her nose and she was the first to speak.

"Mrs. Botti, what happened then? How did you come to America?"

Mrs. Bottigheimer was surprised that the child had called her *Mrs. Botti* and started to correct her, but she bit her tongue, recovered her composure, and said, "That is enough for now, child, you need your rest."

Marie had thought of Mrs. Bottigheimer for so long as "Mrs. Botti" it was the most natural thing in the world to call her that and she never called her anything else, nor ever wondered why she shouldn't.

For her part, Mrs. Bottigheimer just helped Marie have a nice warm sponge bath and dressed her in a freshly laundered night gown, smelling of the same spring flowers as her pillow. She kissed her on the head, tucked her tenderly into bed, pulled the shade and left the room, chuckling to herself at the new name she'd acquired. Mrs. Botti indeed!

Marie hadn't realized how much her leg had been throbbing until she found herself alone.

Until the aspirin Mrs. Botti had given her earlier finally did its work, she pondered on all the things she had told her. She thought about Al's letter and his mention of the resurrection. The missionaries had taught about that too! Would Al come back to Berta?

As she lay there she tried to recall the face of her Grandpa Daddy. It looked too much like Mr. Hansen and she realized sadly she couldn't really remember what he looked like anymore. Could he come back? Could she throw her own arms around her dear Grandpa Daddy again?

Marie had not been taught to say her prayers, but today she fervently asked her Heavenly Father if these things could be true. A feeling of great joy swept her heart as the sweet answer came—they would come back, Albert and Grandpa Daddy, too!

As she lay in the sweet softness of Mrs. Botti's bed, surrounded by the Love of the Lord, she fervently hoped it would be very, very soon. Maybe next month, or next year! She felt so incredibly comforted to know she would see Grandpa again!

Maybe her mother *would* come back and take her home again, like Mrs. Botti said. As she drifted off to sleep feeling warm and safe, she wondered how she ever could have been afraid of nice Mrs. Botti!

Chapter Nineteen

Between her aching leg, her emotional exhaustion and the pain pills Mrs. Botti had given her, Marie slept most of that day and through the night. The next morning began much as the first had, with bright winter sunlight filtering through the enchanted fairy trees—and a big, delicious breakfast.

After Mrs. Botti again fussed in the kitchen and came back breathlessly into Marie's room she heaved herself into her rocking chair and pulled out another little garment to begin stitching on. As Mrs. Bottigheimer hoped she would, Marie looked very interested.

"What is that you're sewing Mrs. Botti?"

"Now, I thought you would never ask. You would like to see my dolls, ja?"

"Dolls?" As Marie asked the question she vaguely remembered the note Mrs. Botti had sent when she made the gift of Grimm's Fairy Tales. It said something like, "Do you like dolls?" Marie was very curious by now.

"Ja, my dolls." Mrs. Bottigheimer labored up from her chair and went to the closet. She pulled out two small crutches and stood with them by the bed.

"This will be a good time to learn to valk with your crutches—come."

She motioned for Marie to get herself up; Marie lifted

and pulled on her cast, swinging it over the side of the bed. Mrs. Botti placed the crutches under her arms and steadied the young girl as she adjusted to them. She took a few tentative steps, the way Mrs. Botti directed, then quickly felt adept as she circled the small room. She followed Mrs. Botti into the adjoining room.

Marie's eyes nearly popped out of her head as she took in what was intended to be the small living room of the tiny house. The room was filled with dolls! They were lined up very lady-like, sitting on the couch as though waiting for tea to be served. Dolls were standing mysteriously on every available table and nick-nack stand. Marie found out later they had small metal stands underneath their clothing which held them up, but when her eyes first beheld them, she was certain they were bewitched!

As if that was not enough, on the other side of the room a very large glass curio cabinet filled the adjoining wall. Marie could scarcely take it all in—behind the glass doors were shelves and shelves of even more dolls! Maybe Mrs. Botti was not a wicked witch, but now Marie was convinced she must be some kind of fairy, for no one could live in such an enchanted place and not be magical!

She was drawn to the curio cabinet that was almost as large as the school library. She let out a little exclamation of joy as she recognized some of the dolls. On one shelf stood Snow White holding hands with all Seven Dwarfs! Behind them was the sweetest cottage, made out of . . . china—yes softly painted fine china! The next shelf held Cinderella, complete with her prince and wicked stepmother and sisters! Beauty and the Beast, the Frog Prince, the Old Woman Who Lived In A Shoe with her whole brood were there, plus many more.

In wonder she gaped until she could gape no more, then turned to look at Mrs. Botti with wondering eyes full of questions.

"I made them, all of them."

"You made them? How?"

"Well, I have a kiln."

Marie said nothing, for a kiln was as foreign to her as a trip to Mars. Mrs. Bottigheimer, seeing her bewilderment, just laughed and explained further.

"First I take some clay and mold it into my dolls heads, arms and legs."

As Mrs. Botti explained, Marie turned to notice a good-sized table in the corner of the room. She hadn't noticed it until now, so overcome was she by the sight of *all* the dolls. On it were some of the strange things Mrs. Botti was talking about.

"Then I make plaster casts of each piece so that I can make the same doll many times if I choose. If you look closely, Cinderella's face is the same as Beauty's." Mrs. Bottigheimer winked at Marie, and said, "You let that be our little secret, OK?"

Marie thought suddenly how beautiful Mrs. Botti was in that moment she winked and smiled. How strange, she thought, in that flash of a moment it was as though Marie had been allowed to see the lovely princess trapped inside Mrs. Botti. Marie would never look at her again with the same eyes.

"After I've made the plaster casts, I pour slip into them and let it sit for about ten minutes and then pour most of it back out to be used again."

"What's slip?" asked Marie with a perplexed look.

"Vell, little von—slip is liquid porcelain."

"What's porce—lin?"

"Vell, . . ." Mrs. Bottigheimer reached across Marie and lifted Cinderella from the curio cabinet. "Marie, touch her face; isn't she beautiful?"

"Oh yes!"

"Vell, this beautiful skin is not soft like yours. It is made of porcelain. Some people call them China dolls. She is similar to the fine china we eat on."

Mrs. Bottigheimer smiled at Marie and continued. "Slip is just her pretty china face in liquid form. I pour it into the mold and after the slip has dried enough, I remove the mold, clean the seam and fire it in the kiln."

"What's a kiln?"

"Come vith me, little von."

Marie followed her into the laundry room and there, next to the washing machine, was what Marie thought was another, funnier-looking washing machine. Mrs. Bottigheimer walked over and lifted a lid that looked like it was made of plaster or cement.

"This is my kiln. Come see inside."

Marie stood on a stool close by and peered into the brick-lined interior. She was surprised that this was a kiln. It looked something like her mother's wringer washer, except that it had shiny, hexagon-shaped metal sides and stood on squatty six-inch legs.

"Mrs. Botti, do you wash the dolls in here?"

Mrs. Bottigheimer chuckled loud and long before she could reply, "No, little von—certainly not; this is where I fire the dolls."

Marie looked at Mrs. Botti like she was crazy. She had to wonder, for just a moment, if maybe she was a witch, after all.

Mrs. Bottigheimer laughed again as she explained, "Firing means to bake the dolls. This kiln is like a big, hot oven."

Marie gasped as she thought, "Just like Hansel and Gretel, here I am—alone in a Ginger Bread House!"

But as she looked into the round, kind face of Mrs. Botti, Marie sighed, relaxed and continued to listen. Something about this lady just felt safe!

Mrs. Bottigheimer talked on, "It makes the slip turn into glass. After I paint them I fire them. I fire some of my lovely dolls' faces again and again to make them so beautiful!" she said with pride as she reached into the kiln and removed a head, arms and legs.

"Do you recognize these?"

Marie just shook her head no. Mrs. Botti chuckled and flashed her another smile. "No matter, little von, you will, you will, all in good time, you will!"

Mrs. Botti said it as though she was a little child planning some wonderful surprise for someone she liked very much. Her enthusiasm made Marie tingle with curiosity for a moment, in spite of the depression that still threatened her with its dark grip. This woman and her house were so full of surprises and wonders.

Mrs. Botti took the little porcelain body parts and waddled back to her sitting room with Marie clumping on her crutches, close behind. She set them on her table and picked up some fabric that was cut in a curious shape. She explained to Marie how this would become the dress for the tiny new doll she would make. Marie could not imagine how that funny shape could turn into a miniature dress and decided it would just be more of Mrs. Botti's magic!

Mrs. Bottigheimer removed her lovely lady dolls from

the couch and set them on the floor against the curio cabinet. She left Marie without a word, and came back in a wink with pillows and a blanket. She made Marie comfortable on the couch, with her broken leg propped high on a pillow—and left again.

Marie looked around this wondrous room in awe. She should have been thrilled with the wonders of it, but her depression and disappointment were still very raw. This time Mrs. Botti came back with a very large bowl of ice cream! She handed it to Marie with a smile, which Marie heartily returned, then settled herself behind her table and took up the tiny garment with needle in hand.

"Would you like me to read you a story—Snow White maybe, while you finish your ice cream, little von, ja?"

Marie wanted very much for a story, but not the story of Snow White. She was too timid, however, to say what she wanted.

But her heart was not so hard to discern and Mrs. Bottigheimer replied, "You do not vant Snow White?"

Marie shook her head in the affirmative. Mrs. Bottigheimer guessed she did not want a fairy tale just now, but she teased for awhile just the same.

"Cinderella? That is my favorite. Or, Hansel and Gretel—but that von is so scary."

Marie didn't dare say no, she just looked at her ice cream bowl and got very busy stirring it. Had she looked up she would have seen the twinkle in Mrs. Bottigheimer's eye.

"So—what do you want to hear?"

Marie jumped at her invitation and stammered, "Ah—could you tell me more about you, Mrs. Botti? How did you get to America? Where is your sister?"

"Ah—yes, my dear Branca, yes . . ." The twinkle faded from her eye and she got a very thoughtful, sad expression. For some time the room was very silent. All that could be heard was the tick-tock of the grandfather clock in the hall and the clink of Marie's ice cream spoon.

Finally Mrs. Bottigheimer seemed to rouse herself and said, "Vell, as I told you before, my Branca came to America and married her Frank. He brought her to this very town we live in now. Her letters were filled with happiness.

"If only our parents would forgive her and communicate with her, she said she would have been the happiest woman on earth. She not only married her Frank, but she became a Mormon too. I never told our parents, for the news would have saddened them too much, although I suppose they knew. I felt very concerned that she had become involved in this strange religion, but she seemed happy, what could I do?"

Mrs. Bottigheimer shrugged her shoulders and laid down her sewing. She folded her ample arms across her work table and leaned closer to Marie as she continued.

"Well, after my Albert died, I lost all hope. I could never look at another man again. My mother, she worried and nagged at me. She constantly invited other young men to the house to dinner. She even paid von very fine-looking man to paint the house." Berta's eyes lit up a bit and she gave a deep chuckle.

"He was constantly bombarded with stories of her Berta. Oh, her Berta could cook and sew and clean. Oh, her Berta was a nice girl. Oh, her Berta loved the little von's, and on and on. The poor man finally brought a very beautiful young woman to work vith him von day. He introduced my mother to his fiance. Well, I laughed and she turned bright red—served her right!" Mrs. Bottigheimer chuckled again.

"Well, von day I woke up and found myself old," she shrugged her massive shoulders and laughed, "and fat—so who would marry a fat old widow? My mother lectured me about it, even on her deathbed, ah, but she did love me—she and papa!

"Well, after they died I kept the old home. None of my brothers cared to stay. Papa left enough money for me to live frugally on. I didn't want for much except to buy lots'a food," she chuckled, "—and slip for my kiln. I used to sell many dolls at a small gift shop in the old neighborhood; it helped to buy ice cream!" Mrs. Bottigheimer chuckled again, quite pleased with herself.

"Well, as these years went by, my Branca—she never had babies. It vas very sad. My mother said it was because she had disobeyed her parents and her God. I did not judge, for why had my Al been taken? I had tried to obey both parents and God!

"Well poor Branca's Frank, he was kilt in an auto accident. She pleaded with me to come to her in America! Of course I came, as soon as I could sell the old home, but it took nearly a year. Well, it vas a good thing I came too, for my dear, dear Branca . . ." Mrs. Botti's voice cracked as she reached into the bosom of her dress for her handkerchief.

"My dear, dear Branca—she did not tell me she had cancer. By the time I came, she was so sick—so very sick." Mrs. Botti's voice broke again and she sniffed as she finished, "It was so good to have her say that last night 'I love you Berta,' and I loved my Branca too!"

Mrs. Botti looked up to see Marie's young round eyes filled with tears. She quickly gave her a kleenex and felt bad she had made the child sad again. Oh what could she do to bring more joy into the life of the little von? How unfair and hard life could be, at least she'd had a protected and wonderfully happy childhood. Again, she determined to try and do something for this little von!

At that moment Marie's heart was completely in tune with Mrs. Botti's. She suddenly felt very guilty for being so sad and depressed about her broken leg and felt very sorry for this wonderful woman, whom all the children called a witch, and who had no friends. Mrs. Botti's life had been a very sad one; at least Marie had made friends here. Marie determined right then and there to try to do something to help Mrs. Botti make friends and be happier!

Chapter Twenty

Marie spent the next two weeks with Mrs. Botti. During this time their friendship and affection for each other grew. Young Marie was hungry and eager for love, affection and attention. Berta Bottigheimer, with all the time in the world and plenty of love to give, gave generously.

Berta Bottigheimer realized that she could only keep this "little von" for a few weeks. Try as she might, she could think of nothing else to ease the child's way, so she determined to shower her with attention, good food and love while she was here.

Marie racked her brain for something to give Mrs. Botti to help her be happier. One day after her nap, Marie went in search of Mrs. Botti. She searched in the kitchen, the sitting room, the laundry room and finally peeked into Mrs. Botti's bedroom. This was the one room in the house she had never been in.

Mrs. Bottigheimer was busily folding and putting laundry into her open drawers. She looked up with a very large smile for the little von leaning on her crutches in the doorway.

"Marie, you are awake, come in, come in—sit here on the chest by my bed, while I finish this little task, ja?"

Marie gladly did as she was told; as she sat on the chest

at the foot of Mrs. Botti's bed her eyes wandered about the room with interest. Every room in this immaculately clean home was of immense interest to Marie. She could not help but to compare it to her step-grandmother's home.

Like Mrs. Botti, her step-grandma Giovanni was a very good housekeeper—everything in both homes sparkled with cleanliness. Like Mrs. Botti, she was an enormously large woman. Fat—she had called her step-grandmother, but that word seemed ugly now; she just could not think of Mrs. Botti in that way.

Though her step-grandma and Mrs. Botti were alike in a few things, they also differed immensely. Grandma Giovanni had passionately disliked Marie; she could not remember a pleasant word or smile of approval for anything she had ever said or done. But Mrs. Botti had nothing but love and praise for her.

"So—has the cat got your tongue, little von?" Marie jumped at the sound of Mrs. Bottigheimer's voice.

"No—I was just thinking how different you are from my step-grandmother."

Marie went on to explain how alike, but different, they were, and said, "Mrs. Botti, I thought all fat people were mean; that is the biggest reason I was so afraid of you."

"Yes, well child, it is good to learn that lesson in life. You should never judge people by those things, not by their weight, or height or color, or even by whether they are rich or poor. People are not black or white, but they are either good or bad. Remember that inside even an ugly beast may reside a handsome prince."

"How can you ever tell Mrs. Botti?"

"By the things they do little von. If an ugly beast does ugly things, then you can be sure he is a beast—by 'their fruits' ye shall know them. If the ugly beast does beautiful things, then he is a handsome prince. Remember, little von, judge people by the things they do; but remember they can also change, just as in the story of Beauty and the Beast. At first the beast was a beast, but Beauty's kindness and love changed him. Always give people a chance to change, Marie."

As Marie soaked it all in, her eyes continued to roam this neat and pretty room. Suddenly it occurred to her that this was the only room without a zillion dolls—just two. Standing on the top of Mrs. Botti's chest of drawers were the most beautiful dolls Marie had seen yet.

"Who are they, Mrs. Botti?" asked Marie pointing to the lovely bride and groom dolls.

"Well now, I thought you might ask," said Mrs. Bottigheimer as she cocked her head and looked lovingly, longingly at her dolls.

"That is my Al and me."

"But?"

"But, I am not so young and skinny as the bride? Well, I was the day I married Albert Bottigheimer!"

"Like you will be when you see Al again!"

Mrs. Botti did not respond and Marie looked back at her; she read something in Mrs. Botti that troubled her.

"Don't you believe you will see Al again? . . . Be resurrected like Al said in his letter?"

Mrs. Botti sighed and looked at the beautiful, trusting, faithful child before her as she measured her words, "Well, little von—it was such a long time ago. The fairy tales that Al believed in, they are wonderful it is true. They are wonderful for von so young as you. I want you to believe in their message of hope, you are so young—but I am an old woman. I—I would like to believe . . ."

Mrs. Botti had finished her task and closed her drawers with a briskness that Marie recognized. Her manner said this subject is closed, as she turned and left the room. Marie was left to stare at her retreating form in wonder.

She looked up again at the beautiful bride and groom doll and realized something that one so young would not normally know. Because her world had not turned out right, Mrs. Botti had retreated into a make-believe world, a lonely world of fairy tales and dolls.

Marie thought about the letter her Al had written just before he died. He had spoken of Jesus Christ and his hope in Him that he would live again and be with his Berta! When Mrs. Botti had first read that letter to her, Marie's heart within burned, in the same way it had when she had listened to the missionaries—in the same way it had when she had listened to her primary teacher.

And when she had prayed about it, she knew the Lord had answered. "It's true, it's true," her heart again insisted, "it's true!" Marie knew, but she realized that Mrs. Botti did not.

Marie realized how knowing these things were true, had made everything else seem unimportant, all the bad, all the sorrow, just didn't matter when you knew!" I have to tell Mrs. Botti," she determined." I have to help her understand and then she won't be so lonely anymore!"

Chapter Twenty-One

Marie was sorry to say goodbye to Mrs. Botti, but she was so relieved the day her mother came to take her home. As usual Emma didn't say anything as she carried Marie down the snowy, icy lane toward home. But that was enough for Marie; she just held on tight and savored the sight and smell and closeness of her mother—who was taking her home!

Marie was sorry the opportunity to tell Mrs. Botti about the gospel hadn't come. But Marie was undaunted; she felt a great peace and sense of "all is well" and with Christmas coming, she had a plan.

Back in school, Marie found herself the center of attention and for once she didn't mind. Try as he might to put her down, Jack Carlson couldn't get anyone to make fun of Marie. No one they could ever remember, even Jack, had broken a leg before. Her big white cast was quite a curiosity. She was pelted with questions: "Does it hurt? Does it itch? Is it heavy?"

Mrs. Jemison gave the children time that first morning to sign her cast. The girls drew colorful hearts and flowers all over it and the boys even signed it too, all except Jack.

He was really chafing over the loss of attention. Marie couldn't help but notice him stewing in the corner while she had center stage. She would not have been human if she hadn't been glad! After all, if it weren't for his big, stupid dog, Marie would still be dancing in the Christmas Pageant.

She decided to be on her guard because Jack would be planning something to humiliate her, that was for certain. Just before recess Jack started in.

"Too bad you can't run and play outside; guess you'll just stick your nose in a book, huh *EDNA*," he whispered as he left with his gang for recess.

That did it for Marie. She slammed down her book, swung her crutches in gear and headed for the coat rack. Outside she became the center of attention again as all the children watched in amazement. At the foot of the slide she hiked her crutches over her shoulder and up the ladder she hopped, on her one good foot. Then down the slide to a perfect landing. At the bottom she looked for Jack Carlson and, sure enough, he was watching.

He looked at her with disdain and said, "So what—any Jack Mormon could do that!"

Marie surprised him by retorting, "Jack Carlson I am NOT a Jack Mormon. I go to primary just like you do and I intend to be there every week. Don't you ever call me that again!"

Jack Carlson was astounded. For once he was speechless. Marie was the first to turn away and headed for the swings. Her big heavy cast actually gave her more momentum as she used it to pump herself higher and faster than any of the other children.

The next day she was using her crutches like ski poles to race Jack Carlson across the street to Primary! As they catapulted her to victory, she glanced back to gloat at Jack. Instead of sulking and saying something insulting, he actually acknowledged that she was pretty good with those crutches!

Would miracles never cease? Here she was looking at the beast and seeing a glimpse—mind you just a bare glimpse, but a glimpse nonetheless—of a real person inside. Marie could never go so far as to say that Jack Carlson might be a prince, even a prince in disguise! Still, that one truly admiring look and comment from her old arch enemy almost made her broken leg worth it!

Mrs. Jemison's plan to include Marie in the play was the second best reason to make her broken leg worth it, too. She told Marie that they decided to dress her as a beautiful angel in her niece's lacy white prom dress, which would flow to the floor covering her cast, even as she sat on a stool. They would curl her hair and wreath it in white and silver tinsel and she would ring a bell signaling the end of the program until curtain call.

She really felt special, even though she was not so naive that she didn't know her part lacked real significance in the play—except to make her feel needed. It was kind of Mrs. Jemison and Marie was flattered and it would be wonderful to feel like a fairy princess all dressed up and beautiful. It was still very hard and disappointing to know she would not be dancing. Still, she squared her shoulders and prepared to be the best angel-bell-ringer she could!

Her mind was far more preoccupied with the surprise she planned for Mrs. Botti. She just had to find a way to give her the gift she so wanted her to have. She planned to give it to her the night of the Christmas Pageant, since Marie didn't know if she would see her on Christmas.

After Primary she found her mother patiently waiting outside in the cold to help her walk home. She coaxed her into waiting a minute more while she went into Mr. Hansen's store.

"Hi, Mr. Hansen!"

"Hey, Marie. Heard you was gettin' around on them there crutches of your's purty good. What brings you in here on a snowy day like this?"

"Well, I have to hurry; my mother's waiting outside. She has to help me get to school and back now."

"I heard that, too. It's a mighty fine mother you have there, Marie. She doesn't seem near large enough to carry a big girl your size."

"Oh, I don't let her either, except over the bridge and a few rough spots like that, Mr. Hansen. I can walk and even run real well on my own!" Marie said a little bit indignantly.

"Oh now, I don't doubt that a'tall—course you can," Mr. Hansen said soothingly as he smiled to himself and thought, "Even little women were still *women*—touchy—cute, but still touchy!" Then to change the subject, he quickly asked, "Now what brings you in today? Need some bread?"

"No." Marie groped for words to tell Mr. Hansen of her desires. "I. . . I need to buy a book—only . . ."

"You don't have the money?"

"No," Marie said dejectedly. Looking up at him and pleading for understanding she rushed on. "I don't want it for myself; if I did I just wouldn't have it, that's all."

Mr. Hansen prodded her a little, "Is it for a friend—a gift?"

"Yes," gushed Marie.

"Well now, honey, I don't sell books," said Mr. Hansen sorrowfully. At Marie's look of dejection he went on,

"Now maybe I could pick you up one in Evanston next month on my regular buyin' trip."

Her look of hope faded when she heard *next month*—that would be too late! She managed to give Mr. Hansen a smile as she thanked him for his kindness and went out to her mother waiting in the cold. Well she would just have to think of another way, and it occurred to her that it wouldn't hurt to pray for it, too. If the Lord could help her find her way home in a storm, He could help her buy a book.

When they got home a car was just pulling out of their lane. As they approached, it slowed and stopped. Marie was certainly surprised to see Sharon's mother, Mrs. Pace, roll down her window.

"Mrs. Giovanni, I'm Sister Pace, an—well it was my turn to take some clothes and things to the D.I. in Evanston. Our Ward—well the folks is mighty generous and we do that every six months or so, you know, to help those less fortunate than ourselves.

Well, it's a long drive and I was thinking since they are for the poor and all, as what you folks might as well have them as not. So I've left a box on your porch."

She cast a disdainful look up and down at Marie and her mother, then added, "I'm certain you'll be right grateful to the good people of our town. Good-day."

With that she rolled up her window and sped away, the tires of her car seeming to add a final insult by flipping dirty snow all over them. Emma's shoulder's sagged a bit lower and Marie's hopeful mood evaporated. They trudged the last stretch home in silence.

Emma dutifully carried the box inside and after removing her coat she began sorting through its contents. Insulted as she was, she could not afford the pride of throwing anything out. Most of the things were very worn, but she was grateful to find some little boy's trousers that seemed to be in fair condition. Her little boys were wearing theirs to threads.

She saw a few dresses somewhat Marie's size and called her in to try them on. Marie was not interested; she had more important things on her mind, but her eyes did light up to see one dress. It was exactly her size—definitely a rare plus, and it was quite pretty too.

As she left the room to try on the dresses, she heard a thump behind her. She looked back to see her mother toss a book onto the table. Curious, she picked it up. Marie's heart began to pound, she couldn't believe it! The very book she had been looking for. Why, she hadn't even prayed for it yet—imagine!

Chapter Twenty-Two

The big night had finally come! Marie, her mother, little brothers and baby sister were almost the first ones to arrive at the church. Mrs. Jemison was there and so was her niece, Miss Jane. She swooped down on Marie like a big bird and hurried her into the bathroom to begin her transformation. She looks just like Mrs. Jemison, Marie smiled to herself.

Miss Jane brushed and rearranged and tried to manage Marie's curly, cotton-candy hair, which was already squeaky clean. Marie had lugged out the washtub that afternoon and insisted that her mother help fill it with nice warm water for her bath. For once Marie had been grateful that the tub was so small; it was easy to keep her broken leg out of the water—it stuck straight up!

Miss Jane arranged the tinsel in Marie's hair and added some tiny, dried pink flowers with baby breath. She stood back and admired the girl. She had seen Marie before around town and had thought her a sorrowful waif, but tonight she was astonishingly transformed. It wasn't that her features were any less plain; she just seemed to glow from the inside—right out to her unusual hair which was a lemon-colored glow. Miss Jane smiled as she turned Marie around to look at herself in the mirror. Marie's eyes registered wholehearted approval!

Then Miss Jane brought out the beautiful dress Marie would wear. She pulled it carefully over Marie's head exclaiming to herself, "I should have put the dress on her first before I did her hair, dad-burn, careful—care-ful!"

Marie nearly laughed out loud at this funny lady helping her. Finally the task was done and after tucking and flicking a few wayward curls, she stood back and clucked a little at the very large dress on the very small child. She rushed off for an instant, then swooped in again with a big box of pins.

She pinned here and she pinned there, she tucked and tugged and walked around and around Marie, clucking to herself all the while. It was all quite entertaining! Finally she had Marie pinned and tucked into the dress to her satisfaction.

She turned the young girl to the mirror and asked, "So miss, how do you like it?"

Marie just stared at the strange cherub looking back at her in the glass. She was beautiful—the thought came immodestly before she could realize it was indeed herself. She was even more beautiful than the vision she had of herself in her imaginary portrait, sitting on her beautiful imaginary vanity in her lovely imaginary bedroom at home! This was not a dream, she was really here! She had never felt more beautiful—and suddenly she was very glad she had broken her leg!

"Oh, Mrs. Botti," Marie whispered, "I do believe in fairy tales, I really do," and her mind was off on a dream:

She was on the stage ringing her bell in the most angelic of possible, angelical ways. She looked out into the audience and nearly wept at the sight of her adoring family and friends. Her mother and siblings, Mrs. Jemison, Mr.

Hansen, and wonderful Mrs. Botti. Oh, how proud Mrs. Botti was of her fairy princess—Marie!

Her thoughts were interrupted by a snide voice, which yanked her mind back to the present. "Well don't we think we're pretty, Marie Rhinehart! Too bad, you won't be dancing. So rude of you to break your leg. Sharon and I had to have extra practices to change the dance—still Sharon and I do dance so well together. Actually, I think the dance is really better with only two people. I think three is a crowd, don't you Marie?"

Marie's lovely dress seemed to act like armor, deflecting each one of Joan's unkind remarks and her halo of tinsel seemed to protect Marie from the temptation to retaliate. She just flashed Joan her brightest smile, pulled her crutches under her arms and left the bathroom!

Sharon was in the hall and grabbed her for a giant hug.

"Oh Marie, you look gorgeous!"

Mrs. Jemison was not far behind, also chirping her approval. Finally the entire cast was on stage, attempting to maintain a semblance of order and quiet. The auditorium out front was filling up nicely and the parents were amused with the flashes of feet under the curtain, barely suppressed laughter, and the very loud whispered instructions of Mrs. Jemison.

Marie was earnestly listening, as she hadn't been to a final rehearsal yet. She knew she was at the very end, but she wanted desperately to do this right. As she listened, she had a distinct impression that someone was looking at her.

She glanced up to meet the eyes of Jack Carlson. His eyes were usually full of mischief and meanness, with a mean retort just waiting on the tip of his tongue to explode at her. She was surprised to say the least to find a look of absolute wonder and even adoration there.

When her eyes caught his, his face went beet red; he glanced away quickly and looked as if he wanted to melt into the bottom of the stage. Marie knew this was truly a night of magic. It was amazing, to be sure, that he had admired her spunkiness on crutches. But this . . .

Before she had time for further amazement, she realized that Mrs. Jemison was in a dither. Apparently little Ashley Jacobsen was still not here—Ashley was going to play the part of Mary in the manger scene. They were ten minutes from opening and that scene would be on stage the entire evening!

Mrs. Jemison ran out to make a phone call and that really set the children off. Their suppressed talking and laughter made no pretense now. The audience below could hardly visit over their noise.

After a short time Mrs. Jemison came bustling back on stage and headed straight for Marie. She steered her into the corner and presented her problem. "Marie, I know how beautiful you look and how you looked forward to being the angel at the end, but . . ."

As they steered through the throng, down the hall and into the bathroom once more, Marie couldn't believe it! Every time something wonderful in her life happened, something else came along to snatch it away. She tried very hard to hide her disappointment and check her awful tears, as her beautiful dress and tinsel were stripped away.

She took the proffered wash cloth to wipe her lovely rosy cheeks away and wiped her eyes as well. She felt numb as the coarse gunny sack dress was pulled over her head and her lovely clean curls were covered by an ugly cloth of the same material.

As Mrs. Jemison hustled her back on stage she tried to make Marie understand that the angel part wasn't important, but that the show couldn't go on without a Mary. She was the only one who could do the part!

Even the words that she was now the star of the show didn't make her feel a bit better. She felt like the star before—even Jack Carlson had admired her beauty! Not that she wanted him to—she almost hated him, but it felt like a victory for all the meanness he had meted out to her.

As Mrs. Jemison arranged Marie on her bale of hay, she noticed her white cast and pink toes sticking out. She tugged at Ashley's dress, which was too small for Marie in the first place, but it would never cover Marie's toes. Mrs. Jemison stood up. For a long moment, with one hand on her hip and the other holding up her chin, she stared at Marie's broken leg. Marie thought she was looking at it as though it was some kind of awful rodent she was deciding how to smack!

Finally, Mrs. Jemison shrugged her shoulders, out of time and out of patience. Mary would just have to have a broken leg, that was all! As Mrs. Jemison bustled about getting everyone else into place, Marie just about died as she realized that Jack Carlson was Joseph! She refused to meet his eye and she refused to cry. For once she was just mad enough that her tears didn't have a chance!

Mrs. Jemison raised her hand, ready to give the signal to open the curtains, when her eyes again landed on Marie. She bustled over and whispered loud enough to reverberate through the entire hall, "Where's your baby?"

"What?" was all Marie could manage.

"Your baby—baby Jesus?"

Marie just shrugged her shoulders as Sammy the

shepherd tugged on Mrs. Jemison's dress to exclaim, "Ashley was bringing her Tiny Tears doll, Mrs. Jemison."

"Ah, that's right," Mrs. Jemison realized. Ashley was sick and she wouldn't be bringing the doll. Mrs. Jemison panicked for a moment, until she had a sudden idea! She rushed off stage again and returned to the chaos on stage with a bundle, which she placed into Marie's arms with a smile. Then she hushed the children one last time, and gave the signal to open the curtains.

Marie looked down into the face of her precious little sister. The baby, sleeping so angelically, seemed to know what the part required. The play commenced, but Marie did not look out into the audience. She did not look like a sweet, adoring mother, looking into the face of her first-born, either. Instead she looked like someone attending a funeral and felt like a person betrayed.

Life was just too mean! It was unfair! What had she ever done to deserve this? Marie had never, ever felt so "poor me" before! She wanted to scream as she thought of how proud she was going to make everyone tonight! How differently people treated a princess from a poor girl in an ugly dress! How she longed for the adoration and approval, worthy of a princess, and she'd had it for one brief moment—now here she sat in sackcloth!

In her anger she whispered in her soul, "I don't believe in fairy tales anymore, Mrs. Botti!"

Marie felt quite sorry for herself through much of the program. She did not listen to the words spoken and she would not look at anyone's face, but most of all she refused to watch the dances—she didn't trust herself to do that! She yearned to be backstage, dressed in her lovely dress, adorned in tinsel and flowers.

Poor Sharon tried like everything to get Marie's attention, to give her a smile and get one for good luck, but Marie wouldn't look at her—she was certainly *not* a happy Mary. Sharon wanted to be mad at her and tell her to stop sulking, but Marie looked so disheartened that she said a silent prayer for her instead, "Please, Heavenly Father, make Marie happy tonight!"

Mrs. Jemison, watching from the wings, noticed Marie's countenance and felt dismay. She should have considered how Marie would feel about this.

"What have I done to her, she lamented. "I gave her a chance to be admired and then snatched it away! She must be hating me right now."

Into her consciousness came little Nathan Tanner's fourth grade voice, reading the ancient words of the wondrous story with all the feeling he could muster, *"And Joseph also went up from Galilee, out of the city of Nazareth, into Judea, unto the city of David . . ."*

Something wonderful touched her heart and she said a silent prayer, "Oh Father, help Marie to feel the spirit of this night!"

Down in the audience Marie's mother was anxiously watching her newborn, hopeful the babe would not cry, but more concerned that the girl holding the child would not drop her or let her choke or something. As she was trying to pay attention while watching the babe, little Tony kept tugging at her sleeve. She kept brushing him off impatiently, but to no avail.

She finally leaned down and threatened to take him out, when he stood up, pointed at the stage and blurted out for the entire cast and audience to hear, "Mamma, look! Marie is holding our baby!"

The audience laughed and Marie's face turned red; though she didn't flinch—she certainly looked angry! Emma was absolutely surprised to find that it was indeed Marie holding her babe. Well, she visibly relaxed, realizing Marie would be careful with her sister.

"Why was she playing the part of Mary," Emma wondered. Oblivious to the disappointment Marie would be feeling she settled back to listen.

"And so it was, that, while they were there, the days were accomplished that she should be delivered. And she brought forth her firstborn son . . ."

In spite of herself, the ancient sweet words melted some of Emma's depression, softening her heart and her troubles for a brief sweet hour.

Little Tony's outburst alerted Mr. Hansen and Mrs. Bottigheimer that indeed Marie was now playing the part of Mary. Patiently waiting for her part at the end they had not noticed. Mr. Hansen pulled his glasses from his pocket and looked more closely at his young friend. He chuckled as he realized *Mary* had pink toes sticking out from a stiff white leg. His smile faded as he silently whistled through his teeth, realizing her mood.

"She is not a happy lass, that one," he mumbled under his breath. He was perceptive enough to realize she was chafing over not wearing the lovely dress and playing the princess.

He felt sorry for her as he turned his attention again, to the cute little guy narrating, *"And there were in the same country shepherds abiding in the field, keeping watch over their flock by night . . ."* and Mr. Hansen also offered a prayer in his heart for Marie.

Mrs. Bottigheimer sat up and took notice of Marie. "Oh

my poor little von," she thought. Marie's funeral countenance hurt Mrs. Bottigheimer's heart. "She so vanted to play the princess—the angel princess."

Mrs. Bottigheimer shook her head in sorrow, then looked down at the present in her lap Marie had slipped into her hands just before the program started. How beautiful she had looked, exactly like an angel, a Cinderella, a Fairy Princess to be sure! How had they switched her part so quickly?

Mrs. Bottigheimer tried to turn her thoughts back to the program.

"And lo, the angel of the Lord came upon them, . . ." but she felt an incredible urge to open her gift. It was not Christmas yet—would Marie mind? As she thought about the gift she had for Marie it made her wiggle with pleasure to imagine her face when she gave her the porcelain "Marie Doll" she had lovingly made for her.

On impulse she carefully and quietly tore the paper back to find a well-worn, obviously used book. As Mrs. Bottigheimer read the title she instinctively bristled and felt that old, bitter fear, heavy and deep inside. If any other soul on earth had given her this book, she would never have opened it. But the fact that it was a heartfelt gift from an innocent child seemed to guide her trembling hands. Inside on the first blank page was a note from Marie:

Dear Mrs. Botti,

Once you gave me a book too. You told me to believe in fairy tales, but I found out you don't believe them so I am giving you a book that will help you believe them. . .

Mrs. Bottigheimer closed the book and read the title again, fighting with the fear and anger and bitter memories the very name of its title inflamed. Poignant was the memory of that day her Branca had tried to give her this same book!

The words of little Nathan on stage broke into her thoughts, *"And the angel said unto them, Fear not: for, behold, I bring you good tidings of great joy, which shall be to all people . . ."*

Fear not. FEAR NOT! The words echoed through her mind as something infinitely sweet seemed to wash through her very being. Miraculously the pain and bitterness melted into an intense feeling of peace. Could this be? Yes! This was a message from heaven, from God, from little Marie. She continued with Marie's letter,

. . . because I know, this is a true book . . .

Again Nathan's voice seemed loud and clear in her heart.

"For unto you is born this day in the city of David a Savior, which is Christ the Lord. And this shall be a sign unto you . . ."

By now Mrs. Bottigheimer's heart was pounding in her bounteous breast—this was a message from God, He was about to show her, Berta Bottigheimer, a sign!

"Ye shall find the babe wrapped in swaddling clothes . . ."

Just then Marie's little sister let out the tiniest cry and Mrs. Bottigheimer looked up to see her sweet little von gently sooth the babe. As love for this young friend swelled her soul, her eyes filled with tears as her mind heard the words of Marie's note again—*"Because I know this is a true book!"* MARIE was her sign from God. Marie spoke the truth, and she knew it—and she knew that God knew that she knew it!

"And suddenly there was with the angel a multitude of the heavenly host praising God, and saying, Glory to God in the highest, and on earth peace, good will toward men . . ."

Through her tears she finished Marie's note.

. . . And I love you and I want it to make you happy and have friends like I do and I want you to be with Al again and I know you can if you just believe in this book.

Merry Christmas, Love
Marie

Mrs. Bottigheimer removed her lace handkerchief from her bosom and wiped her sniffles. She closed the book and read the title again. Well, how could such a young girl know the Book of Mormon is true? With these thoughts came another phrase of scripture heard so many years ago, *"Out of the mouths of babes . . . "*

She looked again at the young "Mary" her Marie on stage and prayed, oh my little babe, "Please God, help her to feel the wonder of this night!"

Before Berta had uttered her prayer, the prayers of Sharon, Mrs. Jemison and Mr. Hansen had already begun their magic in Marie's hardened heart. Through her anger and disappointment she began to hear the beautiful message, *"For unto you is born this day a Savior . . . "* and feel its power.

Then as little Rose wiggled and yawned and screwed up her face, as though to fuss, Marie gently rocked her until the baby calmed. As Marie looked into her adorable face and felt the peace and joy of tending one so small and helpless, another scripture whispered, *"If ye have done it unto one of the least of these my brethren . . ."*

Marie couldn't help herself then, she began to smile. She smiled over at Sharon and winked at her and, of all miracles, she even looked up at Joseph! It had to be Christmas for Marie to give Jack Carlson a big smile, and it had to be Christmas because he returned it!

Then she smiled down into the faces of those she loved. Her mother seemed happier! She beamed a smile of pride just for Marie! Her little brothers waggled their small hands in greeting. Mr. Hansen's eyes twinkled as always, as they gave her their best wink, and Mrs. Botti's face was filled with wonder!

Something wonderful was happening to Mrs. Botti. Marie looked at her lap filled with the crumpled Christmas paper and saw she was earnestly reading Marie's note. Mrs. Bottigheimer looked up at Marie. Their eyes met—the middle-aged woman and the eleven-year-old girl—exchanging the same message of friendship and love. Both radiating with testimony, joy and hope.

The same white, moving, circling light of the spirit seemed to fill the hall and the hearts of all those who loved the Lord. Mrs. Botti's eyes were sparkling with gratitude for Marie's gift and shining with a wondrous new knowledge!

Marie's eyes suddenly filled with tears of gratitude as she looked around at all those she loved. Unashamed, she smiled up at Jack Carlson one more time!

Marie was too young to understand all the complexities of human behavior. She would be a grown woman before she could consciously comprehend that even in sack-cloth—without the tinsel and lace and pretty hair—she was still loved and admired.

Marie only knew that on that night, she was happy—because she *did* have the best part in the Christmas Pageant after all!

Epilogue

Unable to find words to express the feelings that stirred within her, Dianne sat still for some moments.

Marie too, was lost in her own thoughts . . .

Finally Dianne said, "It just makes me want to hug that little Marie. Life must have been so hard for her—for you! Mom how did you do it? How did you overcome all that opposition? How . . . ?"

For the first time in hours they both heard the clock chiming in the den.

"Oh my dear—I've kept you up all night long. Look!"

Together they watched the gray morning light begin to sift through the dining room window.

"It's almost dawn," exclaimed Dianne shifting in the hard chair. But clutching her robe tighter with a shiver of morning chill she sat still, unwilling to let go of the feelings Marie's story had evoked.

"Mom, remember you said, that your story was filled with sorrow?"

"Yes."

"Well your troubles certainly did seem to outnumber the good times."

Marie got up, patted her daughter-in-law's hand and headed for the door. Then she paused, turned back toward Dianne, and said, "Once, a few years after she joined the church, Mrs. Botti said to me, 'Though life's sorrows may outnumber its joys, the JOY *outweighs* the sorrow!'"

The two women smiled warmly at each other as they shared the consonance of the moment, then Marie quietly whispered, "Goodnight, Dianne."

"Wait! You still haven't told me how you got the fairy tale dolls. They were Mrs. Botti's weren't they?"

"Oh yes, Dianne, to be sure they were Mrs. Botti's—but it is very early in the morning and *that* is another story!"